THE INN AT SEAGROVE

South Carolina Sunsets Book 4

CHAPTER 1

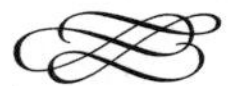

Meg rocked in the chair, the darkened nursery only dimly lit by the moonlight outside the window. Clouds were obscuring most of it, but she could still make out the crib across the room and, of course, the little red light illuminating from the baby monitor on the table nearby.

The room wasn't that big, but neither was the apartment that she and Christian shared with their new daughter, Vivi. Meg wasn't accustomed to such a small space having grown up in a large suburban home. At least the tiny dorm room at the university she attended in France prepared her for living in tight quarters.

Tonight, like most nights, she had hidden herself

away in the nursery even though Vivi was fast asleep in her crib. She wanted to say that she needed to be close to her new baby, but right now she was just trying to get space. She needed quiet. She longed for a peace that just wouldn't come.

When the doctor had laid her new baby on her chest, she'd felt a rush of love she didn't even know was possible. Her cheeks hurt for days because of the huge smile she had plastered on her face every time she looked at Vivi.

And then something changed. At first, it seemed subtle. She didn't want to get up and do her two AM feeding. Of course, she had to since she was breast feeding, but she didn't want to have that bonding time for some reason. She felt disconnected, in a way.

Then there were the days she cried all day long. Her doctor told her that her hormones were all over the place and would regulate themselves soon enough. She felt alone and exhausted.

The few times she'd tried to explain her feelings to Christian, he'd looked much like a deer caught in the headlights. She knew he wanted to help, but most of the time she felt like wringing his neck.

Her emotions just made no sense. She was both panicky and depressed, angry and yet sad. She didn't know if she was coming or going most of the time.

At twenty years old, she hadn't expected to be a new mom. She didn't think she'd be living in a tiny South Carolina town where she knew no one but her family and Dixie. She felt isolated and too embarrassed to tell her mother what was going on. She'd put her through enough getting pregnant so young and out of wedlock.

Every night, before she fell asleep, she prayed so hard that God would make her a good mother. She prayed that He would take these awful feelings away and replace them with happiness and joy. She hadn't felt much joy in the two months since giving birth.

What was a new mother supposed to feel like, anyway? Surely, it wasn't sad, anxious and depressed. Wasn't she supposed to gaze upon the brand new life she'd created and feel a welling up of love and excitement?

For her, that hadn't happened since the first few days after having Vivi. Of course, there were short moments of peace where she stared at her new daughter and thanked God for this wonderful gift. But, there were more times that she wanted to curl up into the fetal position and cry for days.

Her heart broke that this was her first experience

with motherhood and that Vivi wasn't feeling enough love from her. What would that do to her daughter as she grew up? Would this time of her life make her feel disconnected from others or depressed herself one day?

It was all too much.

She sucked in a deep breath and blew it out. The air smelled of baby powder. She could hear Vivi quietly breathing a few feet away and wondered what that kind of peace felt like.

"Hey," she heard Christian say softly from the doorway. He had to know something was wrong. After all, he'd found her crying earlier in the day, holding a dirty diaper in one hand and a pack of animal crackers in the other. She'd been so tired and hungry and worn down that she just froze in place, forgetting that she was trying to eat a snack.

"Hey," she said, not turning around to face him. Instead, she kept rocking and staring out the window.

"You coming to bed soon?"

"I don't know," she said. Part of her wanted to sleep in the rocker. The other part of her wanted to go outside and run until her legs gave out, and she wasn't even a runner.

This push-pull feeling of new motherhood had her stumped. She adored her daughter, but she also wanted to run away. Why was her brain betraying her like this?

Christian walked closer, still keeping his voice barely above a whisper. "Meg, you need sleep. Come to bed."

She looked up at him. "Don't push, Christian."

He nodded slowly and walked out, closing the door behind him. She wondered if he'd leave her soon, maybe even file for custody. She loved him so much, but he didn't deserve this either. Maybe another woman would raise her child better. Maybe she should've done the adoption so Vivi would have a better mother.

As tears rolled down her cheeks like soldiers running straight into battle, she pulled her knees up to her chest and prayed that morning would be here soon.

DAWSON POUNDED the last nail on his new deck overlooking the beach and stood back to look at his handiwork. He wiped his brow and took a long drink from his water bottle. This project had been a labor of love. He hadn't told anyone about his big plans yet, and he wondered what Julie would think.

"Wow! This looks amazing!" she said from behind him.

"Hey, you," he said, smiling. It was always a good day when he got to see her. Her life was busier than ever with Meg and the new baby, Colleen back home and working at the bookstore.

He pulled her into a tight hug and kissed the top of her head. She always smelled like strawberries which just happened to be his favorite fruit.

"I missed you," she said as she looked up at him. It had been a couple of days since they'd seen each other.

"Ditto," he said, stepping back. "So, you like it?"

She walked around the platform deck. "I love that you didn't put spindles up because now you have this amazing view of the ocean. I could sit here all day, every day."

"And you're always welcome to do just that," he said with a laugh. He put his arms around her waist from behind and pressed his lips against her neck. "In fact, we could just stay here from now on, and people can come visit us. We'll have food delivered, and I'll put a portable toilet right over there."

She laughed. "I was happy with this plan until

you mentioned the toilet. Kind of ruined the moment."

Dawson was nervous about telling her his news. Maybe she'd think it was a dumb idea or that it would be too time consuming. After all, they were already struggling trying to find more time together.

"Are you ready for a break? We could go into town and get some lunch," she said.

He scrunched his nose. "I would love to, but I actually have an important meeting in an hour."

She looked at him quizzically. "Is it a doctor's appointment? Are you okay?"

He laughed. "Nothing like that. It's actually with my attorney."

"Oh."

"Aren't you curious why I'm meeting with my lawyer?"

She shrugged her shoulders. "I assume you'd tell me if you wanted me to know."

Dawson smiled. "Well, it just so happens I do want you to know."

"Okay..."

"The reason I'm working on this deck and all of these other projects is because I'm opening up The Inn at Seagrove."

Julie's eyes opened wide as she put her hand over her mouth. "What? Seriously?"

He froze for a moment. Did she think this was a silly idea? Maybe she thought he wasn't capable enough to run an inn.

"Yes, I'm serious," he said.

Julie grinned and jumped up and down before hugging his neck tightly. "Oh my goodness! Congratulations, Dawson! That's so amazing!"

This was one of the things he loved about her. She always supported him no matter what.

He pulled back and looked at her, his hands around her waist. "Really? You're happy about this?"

She looked at him, confused. "Why wouldn't I be?"

"Well, it's going to consume a lot of my time, so we might not be able to go out as much. And, to be honest, I thought maybe you'd think I was crazy being a man trying to run an inn."

She smiled and put her arms around his neck. "Dawson Lancaster, I believe you can do anything, and I support you no matter what."

"You're amazing," he said, kissing the top of her head.

"And I'll help you in any way you need me," she said.

Dawson chuckled. "I may just take you up on that. So, have you seen Vivi today?"

He always poked fun at how many times Julie snuck away during the week to see her new granddaughter. She was obviously madly in love with her chubby little cheeks and wispy brown tuft of hair.

"Not today," she said with a sly smile. "I called Meg but she sounded so tired that I decided not to invite myself over."

"Is she okay?"

"I think so. Being a new mother is so exhausting. I'm sure she isn't getting much sleep."

"You're probably right about that."

"When are you planning to open this place?"

He sucked in a deep breath and blew it out. "Actually, next month."

"Next month? Really? That's fast!"

"I know. I really want to be up and running for the holidays, though, so opening in October gives us a few weeks to work out the kinks."

"What about Lucy?"

"Oh, she's sticking around to be my in-house chef. Believe it or not, she's excited. She likes having people around."

"I bet your granny in heaven is grinning from ear to ear right now."

"I hope so. I want to make her proud of me."

Julie rubbed his arm. "I'm sure she already is."

JANINE WALKED DOWN THE SIDEWALK, taking in the changes that were going on. The town had recently started building a new gazebo in the square, and a couple of shops had new tenants moving in soon.

She loved parking further away from her studio and walking through town. It was the most quaint place she'd ever been to in all of her travels. Everyone was friendly, warm and welcoming. She truly loved her new home.

The yoga studio was becoming more popular by the week. Even tourists were coming during their vacations, and her on location beach classes were a hit. She had even started working with the local elementary school, doing stress reduction PE classes and teaching the kids about meditation in a way they could understand. Her dreams were all coming true.

And then there was William. Their relationship had strengthened as he worked side by side with her to help make the yoga studio successful. His guidance had helped her become a businesswoman, and she'd never thought that was possible.

For the first time in her life, she found herself looking at a future with a man. She'd even imagined what it would be like to get married and live the white picket fence lifestyle she'd never thought she wanted.

As she walked closer to her studio, she was surprised to see that the space next door had finally been rented after being empty for a couple of months.

"Good morning," William said as he walked up and handed Janine her normal morning cup of coffee.

"Good morning," she said, smiling as she planted a kiss on his cheek. "Thanks for the caffeine fix. I need it."

He looked over her shoulder at the store window behind her. "Somebody rented this place?"

She turned back and read the government sign affixed to the window. "Yeah. Looks like it's going to be a bakery of some kind."

"Yum. I love anything baked," he said, laughing.

"Yeah, I know. You devoured that poundcake Julie made on Sunday."

He smiled. "Hey, it was good. What can I say?"

"She got the recipe from our mother, who got it

from her mother. My Nana made the best poundcakes."

"Well, that's one family tradition I'm onboard with. So, do you have a class this morning?"

"I do. This morning is a seniors class. I love teaching these ladies."

He rubbed her arm. "I'm so proud of what you're doing around here, Janine. I've had so many people tell me how much your classes have helped them. One guy I work with said his wife's sciatica is gone."

She grinned. "That makes me so happy."

"Well, I'd better get to work. My boss said he needs to meet with me this morning."

She furrowed her eyebrows. "I hope everything is okay."

He shrugged his shoulders. "I hope so too. I'm sure it's just to talk about some projects we have coming up next year. I'll meet you for lunch?"

She gave him a peck on the lips. "Can't wait."

"ALL I'M SAYING IS that I'd love to meet him," Julie said, grinning.

Dixie rolled her eyes as she continued digging

into the new box of books that had been delivered to the store that morning. Going into the fall season, they were overrun with cookbooks for the upcoming holidays, even though it was still quite warm and summer-like outside.

"I mean, you say I'm like the daughter you never had. Wouldn't you want your future husband to meet me?" Julie said, toying with Dixie.

"He's not gonna be my husband, darlin'. Johnny was the only husband I'll ever have."

Julie reached up to the top shelf and straightened a row of books about organic gardening. "Never say never."

"Oh, I'm definitely saying never."

Julie blew out a breath. "Fine. Then he's your new boy toy."

Dixie cackled. "Boy toy? Good Lord."

"Seriously, why can't I meet this mystery man?"

Dixie stopped stocking the shelf and looked at her. "Sweetie, it's nothing serious. We're just getting to know each other. When you get my age, you don't get too attached."

"That's sad, Dixie. You should look forward to a long and wonderful life."

She smiled. "I do, hon. I love this life I live."

Julie hugged her. "And you deserve an amazing second love story in your life."

"I didn't say anything about love," she chided.

"Fine. I'll leave you alone about it... for now," Julie said with a wink.

The door chimed, and Julie looked up to see Christian walking in. He looked tired, almost beat down, and it worried Julie the moment she saw him.

"Hey, Christian. Are you okay?"

He shrugged his shoulders. "I'm sorry to bother you both while you're working."

"Aw, hon, we're rarely actually working," Dixie said with a chuckle. Realizing he was serious, she cleared her throat. "I'm just going to do a little work in the storage room. Call me if you need me, Julie."

She made herself scarce as Julie pointed for Christian to sit down at one of the little tables in the cafe area. "What's going on? Is the baby okay?"

"Vivi's fine. It's Meg I'm worried about."

"Meg? What's the matter?"

He sighed. "Honestly, I don't really know." His thick French accent was still taking Julie time to get used to, but she understood most of what he said.

Julie was growing concerned. "What's going on, Christian?"

"I don't want to be overly dramatic, but I'm getting worried. She seems sad a lot of the time."

"Maybe she's just overwhelmed with being a new mother?"

"That's what I thought at first, but I don't think that's it. She's sleeping a lot, but then she stays up all night. She doesn't seem interested in things anymore either."

Julie's stomach clenched. "Do you think she might hurt herself or the baby?"

He shook his head. "I don't think so, but this isn't the woman I know. I've tried talking to her, but she cries, and I hate when she cries."

Julie reached over and squeezed his hand. She felt sorry for him, being in a new country, trying to work a new job and bond with his new baby. He looked haggard, as her grandmother would've said.

"I'm so sorry I haven't been around to help more. I didn't want to intrude, but it sounds like you need backup?"

He smiled slightly. "Yes, please."

"How about if I come by after work and bring some dinner? I'll see if Meg will talk to me. Sound good?"

He let out a breath. "Sounds great, actually. I

think Meg really needs you right now, even if she doesn't realize it."

Christian stood up, and Julie hugged him. She'd really grown to like him since having the chance to get to know him the last few months. He seemed to be a good father, and she hoped he would make a good husband to her daughter one day. She didn't ask about their plans for getting married, not wanting to cause a rift in her relationship with Meg.

As she watched Christian walk down the sidewalk, Dixie reappeared from the stock room. "Everything okay?"

Julie sighed and sat back down. "Not really. Christian said Meg is struggling."

Dixie sat down across from her. "Oh, I surely remember those days."

"You do?"

She chuckled. "I'm not a hundred years old, my dear. I can still remember things, even what I had for breakfast this morning."

Julie smiled. "I didn't mean it like that. I'm just surprised to hear that you struggled."

"Oh my, yes. After I had William, I thought I was losing my sanity. Back in those days, there was no room for women to talk about such things, though. There were times I cried all day for no reason. I was horrible to Johnny too. When I told my doctor, he called me a 'hysterical woman' and told me take a tranquilizer pill. Of course, I never did, but it took me months to feel almost normal again."

"Wow, I guess I was blessed. I never had any issues after having my girls."

"It's a crapshoot, I suppose. Some women do fine and others struggle. They call it..."

"Postpartum depression."

"Yes, that's right. I watched a news report about it years ago. Maybe Meg is struggling with that?"

"I think you're probably right. Listen, do you mind if I leave a little early? I promised Christian I would make dinner for them and bring it over. I need to go to the store and then go home and cook..."

"Of course, darlin'. You take all the time you need."

Julie walked behind the counter and picked up her purse. "Oh, wait. Don't you have a date this evening? I don't want to mess up your plans."

Dixie smiled. "Sugar, what's happening with Meg is more important than a silly date. We'll just go to dinner a little later. No big whoop."

Julie laughed at Dixie's sayings. Some of them

she'd never heard before, and others made her feel right at home. "Thanks. See ya tomorrow!"

As Julie made her way out to her car, she felt a stirring in the pit of her stomach. Was she qualified to help her daughter through this, or were things worse than she feared?

CHAPTER 2

Janine sat at the table, tapping her fingers on the metal surface, as she watched people in the square. William was never late, and her stomach was growling like an angry lion. Teaching yoga classes burned calories like nobody's business, and she'd taught three already that day. The pack of trail mix she'd scarfed down at ten o'clock was long gone.

"Sorry I'm late," William said as he jogged up and kissed her on top of her head. She loved when he did that. It just felt so intimate and reassuring.

"No problem. I was about to start eating this menu, though," she said, holding it up. "Let me get the server's attention." She held up her hand and smiled as she waved at Denitra, their favorite server at the sandwich shop.

"Hey, y'all," Denitra said. "What'll ya have today?"

William told Janine to go first as he quickly looked at the menu. It wasn't like he didn't know what was on it. They ate here practically every day. Yet, he always looked at the menu again, as if something had changed from the day before.

"I'll have a chicken salad pita with chips and a fruit cup," Janine said. "Oh, and sweet tea, of course."

Denitra smiled. "Of course. Is it even a meal without sweet tea?"

"I think not," Janine said, handing her the menu.

"I'll just take…" William started to say.

"A Cuban sandwich with extra pickles, barbecue chips and a sweet tea with extra lemon," Denitra and Janine said in unison, laughing.

"Am I that predictable?"

Janine smiled and reached across the table to squeeze his hand. "Maybe just a smidge."

Denitra took Wiliam's menu and headed inside to place their orders. "What can I say? They have the best Cuban sandwich on the planet."

"You know, I love the predictability of our relationship."

"Oh yeah?"

She leaned over the table and planted a soft kiss on his lips. "I do. Most of my life was spent traveling around, not having real roots. I like knowing where we're eating lunch, what you're ordering, what TV show we're going to binge watch this weekend. It's nice. It's comfortable."

He looked at her for a long moment. "Is that what you want? Nice and comfortable?"

She shrugged her shoulders. "I don't know, but it's great right now. We have our whole lives to be adventurous. I'm just enjoying the monotony for a change."

"Monotony?"

"That sounds like a bad word to most people, but I'm relishing routine now. I love my class schedule, knowing how much money I'm making, having family dinners on Sundays." She noticed he looked distressed. "Are you alright?"

"Janine, we need to talk," he said. Denitra set their drinks on the table, gave Janine a worried look and walked away. Even she knew that "we need to talk" was never a good thing.

"Okay. You're scaring me a little bit."

"You know I adore you, right?"

"If you were going to break up with me, could you have not done it in public? Or were you afraid

I'd punch you, so you figured it was safer in public?" Her face turned red, evidence of her Irish heritage betraying her.

"Janine, relax. I'm not breaking up with you," he said in a loud whisper. She took in his words, trying to will her blood pressure to go back down to a normal level.

"You're not?"

"No, and I never will now that I know you plan to punch me," he said, chuckling.

She took in a deep breath and blew it out. Part of her was really bothered by how quickly she became upset at the idea of him breaking up. She didn't want to depend on a man for her happiness, but that's exactly how it felt in that moment. She would have to work on that about herself.

"So, what do we need to talk about then?"

He cleared his throat and took a long sip of his tea. "I, um..."

"Here ya go. Enjoy!" Denitra said, putting both of their sandwich baskets on the table. She glanced at Janine, obviously wondering if everything was okay. Janine smiled and nodded.

"Thanks," William said as Denitra walked back inside.

She stared down at her food, dying of hunger but

also too anxious to take a bite. "Will, come on. Don't keep me in suspense."

He sighed. "I had a meeting with my boss today. We're opening a new office, and he wants me to head the whole thing up. I'll hire the new employees, get the office space designed and built out, and I'll be responsible for getting it up and running. There will be a VP there to help me get everything up and running, but then I'll be on my own."

"Oh, that's wonderful, William!" she said, smiling, as she finally picked up her sandwich and took a bite.

"Yeah, I mean it's a great opportunity. I'll get a thirty percent raise and a company car. They're even offering me quarterly bonuses if I meet certain goals."

She looked at him. He still wasn't eating and was staring through her rather than at her. "Then why do you look like someone just stole your puppy?"

He put his face in his hands and groaned before looking up. "Because the new office is in Austin, Texas."

Janine froze, her pita falling from her hands and back into the basket, a glop of chicken salad falling out. "What?"

"He said he's been impressed with my work and

the growth I've brought to the office. And even though it's my choice, I got the feeling that if I say no, I won't get any opportunities in the future."

"But, it's Texas. I mean, that's so far away…"

"I know. He said that he also picked me because I'm not married, and I don't have kids, so it would be easier for me to leave."

Janine swallowed hard. "Is that true? Would it be easier?"

His face softened. "Of course not, Janine. Are you serious? I feel like I want to throw up. I had no idea this was happening."

"When would you have to be there?"

"Next week."

"Next week? That's awfully quick!"

"I know. They've already rented an apartment near the new office out there."

"Wow. I don't know what to say. How long would you be there?"

He let out a long breath. "At least a year."

She sat with that information for a few moments. "So, are you… leaving?" She couldn't help but ask him. Her heart had been broken so many times over the years that she just didn't know if she could take it again.

Janine wanted him to say no, of course he wasn't

leaving her and his mother and all of his friends and their cool new relationship. She wanted him to laugh, shake his head, pull her into his arms and assure her he wasn't going anywhere. But that wasn't what happened at all.

"I don't know yet."

He didn't know? What? Their whole relationship started flashing through her mind. Had she just been a fun hobby for him while he waited for his real life to start? Did she care more about him than he did about her? She suddenly wasn't hungry anymore.

"Okay," was all she could think to say, and even that barely came out of her mouth. Right now, she wanted to go home, crawl into her bed and wait for Julie to come home later and feed her bowls of ice cream. Probably not the healthiest reaction.

The other part of her wanted to be proud of William, that he was doing so well at work that they were giving him this huge promotion. Maybe she just wasn't that big of a person because she couldn't summon the words to say that and actually mean it.

"This opportunity is what I've been working my whole career for. The clients we can sign in Austin would put the company in a great position, and maybe even give me a chance at becoming an owner."

She reeled in her emotions as best she could. "That's great, William. I'm very happy for you."

He looked at her. "I didn't say I was going."

"You didn't say you weren't." She crumpled up her napkin and tossed it on top of her food. "I'm not very hungry anymore, so I think I'm going to go." She stood up and draped her messenger bag over her shoulder.

William stood up. "Janine, please don't go…"

She smiled sadly. "I have to. Please."

He sighed and nodded. "I never wanted to hurt you, Janine."

She looked at him without saying anything and then turned toward her yoga studio.

JULIE RAN around her kitchen like a chicken with its head cut off, trying to finish the dinner she was cooking for Meg and Christian. She'd also bought some extra diapers and baby wipes at the store so she could help out as much as possible with little Vivi's needs.

She adored her granddaughter. Now that she was gaining some weight, her cheeks were starting to fatten up a bit, just enough for Julie to give her a big, wet kiss every time she saw her.

As she pulled the meatloaf out of the oven, she tried not to fixate on her worries about Meg. Since she hadn't experienced any kind of depression when her daughters were born, she hadn't really been looking out for it. If that's what Meg was going through, it made her feel like a terrible mother for not noticing sooner.

"Hey. What smells so good in here?" Colleen asked as she came home from work and trotted into the kitchen, her nose in the air like a bloodhound.

"I'm making dinner for Meg and Christian," she said, covering the hot casserole dish with aluminum foil.

Colleen laughed. "So I get nothing unless I have a baby?"

Julie looked at her, not smiling. "First of all, not funny. And second of all, Christian asked me to."

"Really? Why?" She pushed herself up onto the counter, her feet dangling like they did when she was a kid.

"Has Meg acted strangely to you lately? I mean, since Vivi was born?"

"Well, she's tired a lot. We texted a few times this week, but she doesn't always answer my texts. And I invited her to lunch a couple of days ago, but she said she'd been up all night with the baby. Why?"

"Christian came by the bookstore and said she's really struggling."

"Struggling how?"

"It sounds like she might have postpartum depression."

"Oh. Wow. I never even thought about that. I just figured new moms are tired."

"And that could still be it, but Christian is exhausted with all of it, and he asked me to be back up. So, I'm going in with meatloaf in hand."

"Let me know if you think there's anything I can do."

"I will. So, what's your plan for the evening?"

Colleen grinned. "Tucker is taking me on a candlelight picnic on the beach."

"Oh, well that sounds awfully romantic. Things are moving along quickly with you two, huh?"

"I guess you could say that. But, I'm really trying to take it slowly after what happened with Peter."

Julie touched her knee. "You're still young, so you need to take it slowly. Nobody really knows who they are at your age. You need to experience life and get to know a person before committing."

She rolled her eyes. "I know, Mom. Boy, you can really suck the fun out of a romantic date."

Julie laughed. "I'm talented. What can I say?"

JULIE STOOD outside of Christian and Meg's apartment, her arms full of dinner and her knuckles hesitating in front of the big brass door knocker that was shaped like a lion's head. What would she say to her daughter? She herself had never dealt with postpartum depression, so would she have anything to offer?

The weight of the responsibility was almost too much to bear. She had to be strong and guide her daughter out of this dark place, but she had no idea how to accomplish that. Being a mother never ended, no matter how old the child was. There was always a deep longing to make sure her girls were happy and healthy, and watching either of them struggle in life was hard for her.

Realizing that she was going to drop all of the food pretty soon, she knocked on the door and Christian answered. He looked even more tired than he had in the bookstore. He smiled slightly, appreciation written all over his face.

"Oh, hey, Julie! What a surprise!" he said. Julie almost laughed because he definitely wasn't going to become an actor anytime soon.

A few feet behind him, she saw Meg standing there, the baby pulled to her chest and covered with a blanket as she breast-fed.

"Mom? What are you doing here?"

Julie tried to not take offense. Her daughter certainly didn't sound excited to see her, and her face lacked any kind of emotion whatsoever. She looked pale and tired and distant. Julie almost started crying right there.

"Well, I know how it is to be a new parent, so I thought it might be a nice surprise to bring you both some dinner. I made meatloaf. You've always loved it."

Again, Meg stared at her blankly, almost as if she was looking right through her. "Oh. Thanks." She turned and walked over to the sofa and sat down.

Julie glanced back at Christian and saw the look of despair on his face. This was worse than she had anticipated. Her daughter was obviously not just suffering with a little bit of feeling blue. She was struggling in ways that Julie hadn't imagined.

When she thought about the fact that Meg had had her baby so young, she wondered what the whole hormonal process might have done to her still growing body. Even though she was twenty years old now, Julie had never thought of her as an adult. She was a tiny little thing, and she would always be Julie's baby girl.

Christian took the food from Julie and disappeared into the small galley kitchen. Slowly, Julie walked over to her daughter, who was now putting the baby in the car seat carrier that was next to the sofa. Vivi was asleep, obviously having been filled with nutritious breast milk.

Meg sighed and leaned back against the sofa. The news was playing in the background, but nobody was watching it, so Julie reached over to grab the remote and mute the TV.

"How's the baby?"

Meg smiled slightly, obviously forcing herself to seem happy. "She's good. I took her for a check up a few days ago. Right on target."

“And how are you?" Julie asked, wishing she had asked that question first. One problem with new mothers was that they felt neglected by society. People rarely asked how they were doing, and instead focused all of their attention on the adorable new baby.

"I'm fine."

Meg had always been her bubbly daughter, but right now she seemed like a shell of a human being. This went far beyond just being exhausted and getting up at night with the baby. Julie was getting more concerned by the moment.

"Meg, I can tell something's wrong. I'm your mother. How can I help you?"

Meg still stared straight ahead, now at the muted TV. "I don't know. I don't feel... anything."

"You don't feel *anything*?"

She shook her head. "I thought I would feel happy, excited. But all I feel is empty."

Julie stood up and walked over to the sofa, sitting down beside her daughter. She put her arm around her and pulled Meg's head to her shoulder.

"I am so sorry that I didn't notice you were struggling until now. But I'm going to get you some help."

Meg pulled away and looked at her, anger on her face. "Do you think I'm crazy? You think I'm not a good mother?"

Julie was taken aback. "No, honey, of course not. I just think you're struggling with postpartum depression."

Meg stood up. "Don't try to label me! I'm not gonna be put on some kind of mind altering drug to make me normal. Maybe this is just who I am now."

Julie shook her head. "Meg, it doesn't have to be like this. This should be one of the most exciting times in your life. Let me help you. I'll go with you to your next doctor's appointment, and we can talk to the doctor about..."

"Mother, please leave. Thank you for the food, but I can't do this right now."

Julie was shocked. Christian poked his head out of the kitchen, staring at the situation. Julie was his only hope, and now she'd somehow made things worse.

"Meg, your mother is only trying to help," Christian said as he walked up behind her.

"You don't think I know this was a set up? I might be sad and depressed, but I'm not stupid. I know you must've told her to come over here. And after I asked you not to tell anyone about all of this."

"Honey, he was just worried about you. And the baby."

Meg's head swung around, anger in her eyes. "The baby? You think I would hurt my own child?"

"Not on purpose. Maybe just forgetting about her or something like that... I mean, you're mind is a little fuzzy right now."

Meg's eyes opened wide. "You didn't want me to have a baby this young. I get it. That doesn't mean

I'm a terrible mother. You think I would forget my kid? I'm just a little sad right now. I'm exhausted. Why does this have to be a whole big thing?"

"I think you're a wonderful mother. But, I do think you need some help right now. Some support. You have family that wants to do that for you if you will let us."

A stray tear rolled down Meg's cheek. "I'm asking you nicely to leave. Please. I cannot do this right now."

Julie, wanting to burst into tears herself, refrained. She hugged Christian and then tried to hug her daughter, although Meg's arms never left her side. As she walked over to the door, she turned around one more time.

"Meg, you know I love you. I'm here for you, whatever you need. Just don't forget that."

As Julie shut the door behind her, she never felt more helpless in her life. Her daughter's mental health and her granddaughter's first months of life were hanging in the balance, and she had to do something to help them both. She stepped into the elevator, dropped her purse on the floor and burst into tears.

CHAPTER 3

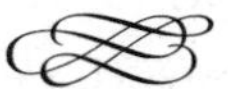

Janine sat on the sofa, the remote control in her hand. After her lunch with William and a full schedule of classes, she needed some downtime. Her plan was to stare mindlessly at the television until her eyes wouldn't stay open any longer. Then she would fall into her bed and try to forget this day ever happened.

A part of her felt immature and ridiculous for getting upset with William for being offered a new opportunity. But the other part of her, which was unfortunately larger, felt betrayed by him even thinking about it.

Of course, he'd said he hadn't decided what he was going to do yet, but if there was even a question then it meant he didn't feel the same way about her that she felt about him. There would be no way that she would ever leave him behind to take another job, so if he was even considering that, she had obviously misunderstood the depth of their relationship.

She dug her hand into the potato chip bag, taking out another handful. If she kept this up, they would have to roll her into the yoga studio. But right now, her appearance just didn't matter to her. There was nothing better than a big bag full of carbs to help with the blues.

Just as she was crunching on the last one and about to put her hand right back into the bag, she heard a knock at the door.

"Oh, good Lord. Who could be here at this hour?" she grumbled as she made her way to open it. She hoped it wasn't anyone important because they were about to see her standing there in her pajamas with a messy bun on top of her head and streaks of mascara down her face. It wasn't that she had been crying, but she hadn't taken the time to wash off her make up before rubbing her eyes.

"Hey," William stood there, hands hanging by his side, like he'd been defeated.

"Oh. Hello." She left the door standing open and

turned back to the sofa, plopping down and picking up the potato chip bag once again.

A moment later, William finally walked inside and shut the door, looking at her carefully before sitting down in the chair next to the sofa.

"You look... comfortable," he said.

She glared at him. "Tread lightly."

He sighed. "Janine, I don't feel good about what happened today at lunch. I think you took everything the wrong way."

"Oh, really? Let me see if I can summarize. Your boss has offered you a cushy new job in a totally different state, and you're considering it. You have a girlfriend here who you claim to love, but you're willing to leave her behind for some extra cash. What am I missing?"

His eyes opened wide. "So that's how you see it?"

"That's how I see it." She dug her hand back into the bag and crunched a chip while glaring at him. She wasn't sure why she did it, except for emphasis.

"You know, I have supported you in your quest to open the yoga studio and make it successful."

"And I have told you a million times how much I appreciate it."

"But now here I am with a huge opportunity, and

at the very mention of me even thinking of taking said opportunity, you're willing to just walk away."

She stared at him before slamming the bag down on the sofa next to her. "Excuse me but I'm not the one wanting to walk away. How in the world do you think we could maintain a relationship when I live on the coast of South Carolina and you're all the way in Texas?"

"I haven't even decided if I'm taking the job!"

"But, you haven't decided that you aren't, William."

"So you just expect me to only take opportunities that are right here in town for the rest of my life? I mean, do you ever plan to leave this place?"

She sat with that question for a moment. Did she? Janine had traveled all over the world for so many years that she had finally realized she never planned to leave Seagrove Island. It had become her home quickly, and her family was there.

"No."

"No? You're never going to leave this place? How can someone who has traveled as much as you have just decide they're never leaving this place?"

"Of course I'll take vacations, William. But I don't plan to ever live anywhere else. Why would I? This is my favorite place on earth. My family is here. I have new friends here. I have a great business here."

William blew out a breath. "Well, I guess that's the difference between me and you. You have everything you want here. I'm not sure I do."

Her stomach clinched. "Then I suppose that is a very big difference between us."

"You know I love you. But, I have to grow as a person and in my career just like you do."

In a way, she understood what he was saying. She didn't like it, but she understood. She couldn't blame him for needing more in his career anymore then he could've blamed her for needing to open the yoga studio.

"So what do we do now?"

"I have to give my boss an answer tomorrow afternoon. I feel like I have to try this, Janine. I have to know whether I'm meant to go up in my company or stay here in Seagrove and build a life."

"William, if you have to even question whether you want to build a future that includes me, then I think you already have your answer."

As they just stared at each other for the next few moments, Janine knew things were never going to be the same. Just like always, she always ended up getting her heart broken in the end.

"I CANNOT BELIEVE what a beautiful picnic you set up," Colleen said. Tucker had gone all out, picking up their favorite foods from the local seafood restaurant. There was just something about sitting right there on the warm sand, the constant breeze blowing through her hair, the last hints of sunlight dancing across the waves. All of it made her feel at peace.

"Anything for the woman I love," Tucker said, smiling at her.

Their relationship had moved so quickly, much quicker than the one she had with Peter. But everything felt right about it. He treated her with so much respect, and they were already talking about future plans like vacations they'd take and where they each saw their careers going.

The "I love you" phase had happened within a couple of weeks of them dating, and she was okay with that because she really did love him. She couldn't imagine a man better than Tucker out there.

"Care to take a walk by the water?" he asked as he cleaned up their spread of food.

"Of course."

For the next little while, they walked along the

water's edge, holding hands and talking about all the latest gossip. Colleen told him about her concerns for her sister, and Tucker talked about the latest toy they were developing at work. It was going to be specifically for kids with sensory issues, like many who have autism.

Without warning, suddenly Tucker stopped in his tracks and stood there. He turned her around to face him, holding both of her hands in his.

"You know how much I love you, right?"

"I do. But you're scaring me a little bit."

He chuckled. "Ever since I met you, my life has been so much better. I can't imagine a future without you in it."

She smiled up at him. "Good because I feel the same way."

And then something happened. After the fact, she couldn't figure out how she hadn't seen it coming. In slow motion, it seemed, he lowered himself down to one knee and looked up at her, a small black box open in his hand.

"Colleen Marie Pike, I will love you for the rest of my life. Will you marry me?"

She froze like a deer in headlights. She tried to muster up the courage to let words leave her lips, but she stood there silently, staring at him like some sort of lunatic instead.

Every girl dreams of that moment in her life, but right now she felt like she was caught in a night-mare. She couldn't get her mouth to work, her legs felt like they might buckle at any moment and she was pretty sure Tucker was feeling uncomfortable by now.

"Colleen?" he repeated.

She cleared her throat, trying desperately to get the words to come out. "What?"

He chuckled, a huge grin on his face. "I asked you a very important question. Will you marry me?"

And then she did the unthinkable. The worst thing ever. The thing no woman ever wants to do.

"No."

JULIE PULLED INTO HER DRIVEWAY, thankful to see her home but still reeling from her visit with Meg. She had stopped by Dawson's house, had a quick bite to eat with him and Lucy and talked more about his plans for the inn.

She had to admit it was good to get her mind off of her daughter for even a short time, although she and Dawson had gone outside, sat by the ocean and talked for quite a while.

She adored him, but his advice was limited. After all, he had never gotten the chance to be a parent since circumstances took that away from him so long ago. Still, he listened and supported her in ways she didn't know a man could.

She thought a lot about what resources she could pull from in the community to help her daughter without losing her relationship with Meg entirely. She knew she had to tread lightly, being there for support but also not overstepping her bounds. It was going to be a very difficult balancing act.

She saw lights on in the living room and opened the door to find Janine sitting on the sofa, her face red and puffy, obviously from crying. She had an empty bag of potato chips sitting next to her and a half empty container of ice cream sitting squarely on her lap.

"Oh no, you're using a tablespoon. That's never a good thing. What happened?" Julie asked as she walked over and sat down beside her.

"I think I broke up with William."

"You think you did?"

"Today, his boss offered him a new job. A better paying, great opportunity type of job."

"That's wonderful! So you broke up with him because he got offered a better position?"

Janine stared at her and then shook her head. "The job is in Texas."

"Ohhh… Now I understand the puffy eyes and the carbohydrate coma you're trying to put yourself into."

"Right. I thought we were doing so well."

"Did he already accept the job?"

"No, but I know that he will. I mean, the fact that he's even considering it means that he doesn't care as much about me as I do about him."

Julie chuckled. "I think you might be reading too much into that."

Julie walked into the kitchen and started to make a pot of coffee, something she knew she shouldn't do so late at night. But she had a feeling that she and Janine would be up for hours talking about this, as she had her own things to worry about too.

Janine followed her into the kitchen, her hands on her hips. "So you're taking his side?"

Julie rolled her eyes. "I'm not taking anyone's side. I'm just saying that because he's considering a fantastic opportunity doesn't mean he doesn't love you."

"Oh really? And how would you feel if Dawson

suddenly had an opportunity across the country and was thinking about leaving you to pursue it? You're telling me that you wouldn't have some hard feelings about that?"

Julie paused for a moment. She could see her point. "Fine. Maybe I would be upset. But perhaps this is the wrong approach."

"What do you mean?"

Julie poured water in the top of the coffee maker and shut the lid. "Maybe by you supporting him, you could use a little reverse psychology and he'll actually stay here."

Janine shook her head. "I'm not into playing mind games anymore. I want a real relationship. I want a house and a dog and stability. I've spent my whole adult life moving all over the world. I'm ready to stay in one place."

"Janine, don't take this the wrong way, but a relationship is about two people. If you get your needs met, but William doesn't, what kind of relationship is that?"

Janine walked back to the sofa and sat down. She picked up the ice cream container and dug out a big scoop, filling her mouth with it. "See? I knew you would take his side," she said, her mouth full.

Before Julie had a chance to answer, Colleen

swung open the front door, slammed it shut behind her and burst into tears.

Julie didn't know what was going on in the air tonight, but she just about couldn't take anyone else's emotional outbursts.

"Colleen, what's wrong?"

"Do we have any more ice cream?" Colleen asked through her tears.

Janine held up the carton. "I'll share. Just get a spoon."

Colleen walked into the kitchen, opened the drawer and took out another tablespoon. Without a word, she plopped down on the sofa next to her aunt and took a big bite.

"Again, Colleen, what's going on? Did you and Tucker break up?"

Colleen shook her head. "No... Actually, I don't know."

"You don't know? Why do I feel like I am in the twilight zone tonight?" Julie said to herself, softly. "Let me try asking this a different way. Why are you crying?"

Colleen leaned her head back against the sofa. "Tucker proposed tonight."

Janine jumped up off the sofa and clapped her

hands. "That's amazing! How romantic! Where's the ring?"

She immediately reached down and picked up Colleen's left hand which, of course, was naked.

"Wait. He didn't give you a ring?" Janine asked.

Colleen sniffled. "I said no."

Janine's eyes grew wide. "You said no? But he's amazing! I thought y'all were really hitting it off?"

"Janine, please," Julie said. Janine slowly sat back down on the sofa and picked up the ice cream container again.

"I really do love him. The future I see is with Tucker, but I wasn't expecting him to propose so quickly. I mean, we really haven't even discussed marriage. I just got out of an engagement, and I... I'm just not ready."

Julie sat down beside her daughter, as she had her other daughter just a couple of hours before, and held her hand. "Did you tell him that?"

"I tried. But he barely said anything. You should've seen him, down on one knee, looking up at me with the little black velvet box and big puppy dog eyes. It was a beautiful ring. He'd set up a whole picnic. He went to so much trouble and then all I said was no."

"Honey, you have to go with how you feel."

"I know, but I think I broke his heart. I don't know that our relationship can survive this."

The three women leaned back against the sofa, each of them with their own brand of inner turmoil. Janine, full of potato chips and ice cream, continued digging in the carton before leaning her head back against the sofa and sighing. Colleen took another scoop, licked it off the spoon and laid her head back. Julie looked at both of them, really wanting to judge them. Instead, she took the spoon out of Colleen's hand, plunged it into the ice cream and took her own bite before laying her head back against the sofa too.

Why couldn't things ever just be easy?

JANINE PICKED AT HER FOOD, barely taking more than a few bites in the thirty minutes they had been sitting there. But Julie couldn't worry about her sister right now. Adult relationship problems were way down on her list of priorities as she sat across from Janine, thinking about her own daughter.

"Maybe I should just drive over to her apartment, pick her up and take her to the doctor. She's tiny. I think I can take her."

Janine chuckled softly. "I'm not sure that's going to be the right approach."

Julie took a sip of her sweet tea. Normally, at least her favorite beverage would make her somewhat happy. Right now, nothing was doing the trick.

"I'm just getting more worried with every passing day. I don't know what to do."

"I think you just have to be there. You have to make sure she knows that you support her, and also that Christian knows he can call on you."

Julie rolled her eyes. "The last time Christian called on me, I think I made things worse."

"Hey, ladies," Dixie said, as she passed by. It was Sunday, so the bookstore was closed, and Dixie looked like she was dressed to impress.

"Hey, lady. Wow, don't you look flashy today," Janine said with a smile.

Dixie was all decked out in a pair of hot pink pants, a frilly white shirt and some of the biggest pieces of jewelry Julie had ever seen. Her make up was perfect, complete with her shimmery pink lipgloss. And her hair, well, it was higher than Julie had ever seen it.

"Okay, you're wearing your best perfume. Where are you headed?" Julie finally asked.

Dixie tried to keep the smile off of her face, but she couldn't. "I have a... little bit of a... date."

"That's great! Why are you being so shy about it, though?" Janine asked.

"Because she has a boyfriend that she doesn't want any of us to meet," Julie muttered under her breath.

Dixie chuckled. "Who says this is the same one?"

Julie looked at her, her mouth dropping open. "You mean this is a different man?"

"Honey, I believe in playing the field! And right now, I've got men on all the bases," she said, cackling.

The thought of Dixie juggling so many dates made Julie smile, both on her face and in her heart. Since getting diagnosed with Parkinson's disease, things had been an up-and-down roller coaster. But once Dixie started going to physical therapy and taking the right mixture of medications, Julie saw the light come back in her eyes.

"Well, well, well... I guess we need to take a lesson from you, don't we?" Janine said.

"Listen, honey, I heard about William's job. I know y'all are going through a rough patch, but my boy loves you. Don't forget that."

Janine smiled and nodded her head. "I'm trying."

Dixie reached down and rubbed Janine's shoulder. “Things will work out. I just know they will."

"Well, if they don't for some reason, I guess you can teach me your ways."

Dixie waved her hand in the air, laughing as she continued walking down the sidewalk. "Better go! Don't want to keep anyone waiting!"

Julie laughed and shook her head. "If we could only be as laid-back as that woman, the world would be a better place."

"True story."

“Hey, what's with this bakery that's opening up next to your studio? Have you met the owners?"

"No," Janine said, finally taking another bite of her sandwich. In fact, I haven't really seen anyone inside other than workers. I'm not even sure when they're supposed to open."

"I'm looking forward to getting some fresh baked poundcake. I hope they have that on the menu. It's the one thing our mother always made well."

"Yeah, she isn't the best cook, is she? But Grandma? That woman made the best biscuits!"

"Yes. And peach cobbler! And chicken and dumplings!"

Janine put her hand on her stomach. "Stop!

You're making me want to gorge myself on all of those things."

“Anything else ladies?” Denitra, the server, asked as she walked up to the table.

“No thanks. But, do you happen to know anything about the new bakery opening?”

“Not really. Just that the owner’s coming from Georgia.”

“Well, hopefully they’ll have some good stuff,” Janine said, smiling as Denitra walked away. “I’ll need the comfort food.”

"Look, I may not know what to do about Meg, but I know what you should do about William."

Janine looked at her. "And what is that?"

"Let him go. If y'all are meant to be together, Dixie's right. Things will work out."

"Yeah, well I've never been really good at not being in control."

"Would you rather have a relationship where William feels like you took away his opportunity? Or do you want him to feel like he has some control?"

"Can't I do both?" Janine asked, with a laugh.

“I don't think so."

CHAPTER 4

William sat behind his desk, trying desperately to keep his focus. He had to finish up the last of his local files before packing up his apartment and making the trip to Texas.

From the moment he had told his boss that he would take the new job, he had second guessed himself. Why was he leaving? He had a great relationship, and his mother who had Parkinson's disease was nearby. There were so many reasons not to go, and he wondered if he was sabotaging himself.

Many times throughout his life, he'd done that. Things would be going good, and he found a way to screw them up. Was he doing that again?

But, there was a deep part of him that didn't want

to admit that he might be meant to live his life in that tiny town. Surely he was destined for greater things. After losing his brother at a young age, he felt the need to do as much as he could with his life to make him proud. He was living for both of them. Did having some big career make him successful? Or did living a life he loved achieve the same thing?

The look on Janine's face when he'd told her about the opportunity had felt like a stab in his heart. He knew he was slamming a wrecking ball through their relationship, but a part of him had hoped that she might say she would come with him.

It wasn't that he wanted to leave Seagrove, but he wanted to feel successful in his career. He just wasn't sure he could do that in such a small town.

He finished up his paperwork, closed the file folder and put it into the box on his desk. He'd packed just about everything, what little he kept in his office. He was a clean freak, so there weren't a lot of knickknacks to take with him on his long trip.

He'd already spoken with his landlord about his apartment rental, and he had a short-term rental set up in Texas. He had no idea if he would be there permanently or not, but on the off chance that he was, he would soon start looking for an apartment there.

All of it had happened so quickly that he hadn't even had a chance to sit down and think about it. And Janine apparently wasn't even speaking to him. The look on her face the last time he had seen her was enough to tell him to stay away from her. He certainly didn't want to be the one to break her heart.

Just as he was gathering up the rest of his things for the walk to his car, he heard a tapping at the door. Figuring it was his boss telling him good luck, he called out for him to come in.

He was shocked when he saw Janine standing there. She had a small brown gift bag in one hand.

"Hi."

He stared at her for a moment. "Hi. I didn't expect to see you."

She smiled slightly. "I figured. Looks like you're getting ready to leave soon?"

He nodded slightly. "In the morning. I was just getting the rest of my things from the office."

"I wanted to come by and tell you good luck."

Now, he really was surprised. "Really?"

She walked over to him slowly.

"Look, I know I didn't take this whole thing very well. But you have to admit it came on rather suddenly, and I didn't have a whole lot of time to process it. "

"Same here," he said, picking up the clock on his desk and putting it into the box. He didn't want to look her in the eye for some reason. It made his stomach feel very uncomfortable every time he looked at her.

He loved her. There was no question about that. He had grown accustomed to seeing her every day, to comparing notes after work, to eating lunch on the square. And now she would just be absent from his life completely.

"I'm sorry, William. I just want you to know that I'm very proud of this new job that you're taking. I don't like that you won't be here, and I will miss you every single day, but I also realize I should've supported what you thought was best for you. This relationship isn't just about me."

He walked around from behind the desk and stood in front of her, only about a foot of space between them. "Thank you. It really means a lot."

“Here. I brought you this." She handed him the gift bag.

He sat it on the desk and opened it up. He pulled out a jar of peach salsa that was his favorite, made at a small mom and pop shop down the street. "One for the road?"

"Something like that. I know you love it, and I doubt you're going to be able to find it in Texas. "

"I think they probably have peach salsa in Texas too," he said, laughing. "But, they won't have this brand. So, thank you."

"Well, I better get going. I don't wanna hold you up from getting ready to leave," she said, looking down at her feet.

"Hug?"

She nodded slightly, not looking him in the eye. This was hard. Harder than he ever imagined it would be.

He wrapped his arms around her and felt her cheek pressed against his chest. Maybe leaving was a bad idea. Maybe he should just stay put and never know what opportunities he may have lost.

All he knew was he didn't want to let her go. He wanted to take everything out of the box on his desk, turn off the light and just stand there holding her as if nothing ever happened. But things had happened. Even if she was forgiving him now, nothing had really changed. He was still leaving, and she still wasn't happy about it.

Without warning, Janine suddenly stepped back, wiping a stray tear away from her eye and forcing a smile. "I meant what I said. I'm really proud of you, William. I wish you nothing but happiness."

She turned and started walking toward the door.

"Janine?"

"Yeah?"

"Are we breaking up? Like, officially breaking up?" He didn't know why he was asking. It seemed pretty obvious, but he hoped he was wrong. He hoped she would say they'd have a long distance relationship for awhile and see how it worked.

She swallowed hard. "I think we have to. Better not to leave things undone."

His breath caught in his chest as he stood there and watched her look at him one final time before walking out the door and shutting it behind her.

What in the world was he doing?

MEG WALKED down the sidewalk slowly, pushing the stroller ahead of her. Christian had left early for work this morning, probably in part because she was driving him crazy.

Every little thing set her off. Sometimes she cried, other times she yelled. She worried that Vivi's first months of life would be full of memories of her mother yelling in the background. But, for some reason, she just couldn't control her emotions.

After her mother's visit the other night, she had been very angry with Christian for what she considered to be tattling on her. In her heart, she knew that he meant well as did her mother. She understood they were only trying to help, but it made her feel inferior.

Having a child at such a young age and disappointing her family had made her super sensitive. The only thing she had wanted was to be able to show them what a good mother she could be. She wanted them to be proud of her, to forget about the disappointments of the past and see her as a grown woman who could take care of her child.

Those first few weeks of motherhood had been tough with late night feedings, a colicky baby, sore breasts and exhaustion on a level she could barely describe. Being a new mother was way harder than she'd ever anticipated, and she had new respect for all of the women who'd gone before her.

She stopped and looked in a store window. It was a baby clothing consignment shop that she'd visited with her mother shortly before the baby was born. She hadn't been in there lately, even though Vivi was about to move up to the next size clothing. She was growing quickly, getting older right before Meg's eyes. Sometimes that made her cry too.

She adored her baby daughter, but there were times that she just felt so empty. Lost. Alone. Defeated. And none of it made any logical sense. She had supportive family all around her. Yet she felt so alone in her misery and sadness sometimes.

Having a new baby was supposed to be exciting. She saw new mothers on TV, in movies and even on the street, and they all looked joyful and happy while she felt like she needed to dissolve into a puddle of tears at any given moment.

She stared blankly into the window, probably scaring the workers inside. As much as she wanted to force herself to walk through the door and purchase something for her daughter, she just couldn't do it. Nothing felt exciting. Nothing felt motivating. Every day it was just the same slow walk through quicksand for her.

She knew that her mother was right, that she should see the doctor. That she should get some help. But, getting help meant admitting that she was the disappointment she'd so feared.

"Are you okay, honey?" she heard Dixie ask from beside her. In her catatonic state, she had completely forgotten the bookstore was right next door to the consignment shop.

"What? Oh, yeah. Hi, Dixie."

Dixie looked at her for a long moment, concern written all over her face. "Sweetie, come with me," she said, taking the other end of the stroller and pulling it towards the bookstore. Meg didn't have the energy to argue.

As they walked into the bookstore, the door shut behind her, and a little bell causing Vivi to stir a bit. She quickly fell back asleep, thankfully.

“Is my mom here?" Meg asked, hoping the answer was no.

"No, she's not. She took the day off to help Dawson get ready for his big grand opening."

Meg nodded slightly. "Oh. That's right. The inn.”

"Sit down," Dixie said. She had such an authoritative voice that Meg didn't even question her or try to argue. She just sat down in the seat and stared straight ahead. Dixie poured a cup of coffee and put it in front of her with some cream and sugar.

"Thanks."

Dixie sat down across from her. "I'm just going to cut straight to the chase."

“Okay…”

"I had postpartum depression."

"You did?"

"I did. I can tell you're struggling something fierce, Meg. But you don't have to. There's help out there for you. Back in my day, there was no help."

"I think maybe I'm just really tired. Vivi hasn't been the best sleeper..."

Dixie held up her hand. "No. Honey, I don't mean to be harsh, but you know as well as I do that this is about more than just you being tired."

Meg's eyes welled with tears. "I've never felt like this before."

"I understand. I really do. When my son was about eight weeks old, I remember Johnny found me curled up in the fetal position, crying beside our washing machine, my cheek pressed to the linoleum floor."

Meg couldn't help but giggle at the image. "Why?"

"I can't remember exactly what happened, but I do know it had something to do with not being able to get a prune baby food stain off of one of his little sleeper suits. I thought it was just the end of the world, ya know? Like it meant I was a terrible momma."

"I get it."

"Another time, I was at the grocery store, and I

realized at the checkout line that I'd left my money at home. I had my baby on my hip and he was just a fussing up a storm. I was so embarrassed that I just broke down in tears and slid to the floor. The poor manager had to get me up and help me to my car while somebody called Johnny at work. I was a mess."

"It's hard to imagine you were ever a mess, Dixie," Meg said.

"Well, I was. A big mess, in fact. But, it got better. You'll get better too, Meg. But, your momma is worried about you."

Meg sighed. "I know. She tried to talk to me the other night, and I lost it. I don't know what came over me."

"Your emotions are all over the place. Who can blame you? Hormones are crazy things. I hate to tell you, but menopause is almost as bad."

Meg chuckled softly. "Oh great. Something to look forward to."

"Well, don't you worry too much about it. You have a few decades before you need to worry about that. But, for now, you have to seek out some help. You can't do this alone. And you shouldn't have to."

"I don't know what to do."

Dixie stood up and walked over to one of her

bookshelves, taking a book off of it. She handed it to Meg.

"We just got this book in the other day. It's all about postpartum depression and some natural things you can do to help yourself. But, in the meantime, your first stop needs to be to see your doctor. And I think you should invite your momma to come with you. She wants to help you, sweetie."

Meg wiped away a tear. "It's just that I have disappointed her so much with all of this, and I wanted to be this perfect model mother. I wanted her to be proud of me."

Dixie's eyes opened wide. "You can't be serious! Your momma is as proud as punch of you! She talks about you girls all the time. And she hasn't been disappointed in you at all. She loves that baby."

"I know she does. But she has to be disappointed in me. How could she not be?"

"Let me ask you a question. Do you love that little baby there?"

She smiled as she looked at Vivi sleeping so peacefully. "With every fiber of my being. I never knew I could love someone so much."

"Is there anything she could ever do that would make you be disappointed in her? That would make you not support her?"

Meg looked at her daughter for a few moments. “Never."

"Mothers are mothers forever. It doesn't matter if they have babies or full grown kids. You are a part of your mother until the day she dies. There is nothing you can do to make her love you any less or be disappointed in you. You’ve got to stop that kind of thinking!"

Meg really did appreciate the way Dixie talked to her. She often wished that her own grandmother, SuAnn, was the same kind of person. But SuAnn was much more critical than she was supportive, unfortunately.

“Thanks, Dixie. What do I owe you for the book?"

Dixie smiled. "Just consider that a gift. Now, you better get over to that inn and see your momma. Set things right.“

"I will. Thanks for the talk."

As Meg walked back out onto the sidewalk, she finally smiled for the first time in a long time. Maybe there was hope. Maybe things could get better. She would have to step out on faith and ask for help if she ever wanted any hope of being the best mom she could. Vivi deserved it.

~

COLLEEN SAT NERVOUSLY at the table. It had been a few days since Tucker's proposal, and they had both done a wonderful job of avoiding each other. She missed him. There was no doubt about that. She wondered if he missed her too or if he regretted the time they had spent together over the last few months. She was encouraged that he had accepted her text invitation to meet for lunch, at the very least.

She tapped her fingernail on the metal bistro table, looking around the square. He was never late, but it was five minutes until noon and he still wasn't anywhere to be seen. Maybe he would get back at her by making her wait and never showing up. After all, she had probably embarrassed him in the worst way possible. It had kept her up for the last several nights as she thought about the look on his face when she said no. They hadn't even gotten a chance to talk after that because Tucker made a hasty retreat, leaving her on the beach to think about what she'd done.

Of course, she couldn't blame him. How nervous he must've been to ask the question, and how shell-shocked he must've felt when she said no. It honestly broke her heart every time she thought about it.

To be honest, she didn't even know why she had

invited him to lunch other than to try to explain herself yet again. She'd texted him a couple of times since the incident, but he had only responded with one or two words. She imagined he must be very angry.

She looked at her phone to check the time again. Three minutes until noon. Maybe he wasn't coming. Maybe she should try to gather up what she had left of her pride and drive back over the bridge to go home. After all, she didn't even really know if she still had a job. As soon as everything had taken place, she immediately used a few of her vacation days to avoid making Tucker feel uncomfortable at work. Why did things always have to be so complicated?

"Hey." She looked up to see Tucker standing in front of her. He was wearing jeans, black boots and a pale gray T-shirt. She loved when he wore T-shirts. It showed off his amazing muscular physique, and right now she wanted to wrap her arms around him.

"Hi. I'm so glad you agreed to come."

He nodded slightly before pulling out his chair and sitting down. He rested his forearms on the table, his hands clasped together. "So, I was surprised that you wanted to meet. I thought things were pretty much over between us."

She looked at him, her lips turning downward into a slight frown. "Are things over?"

"Well, it seems to me that you saying no pretty much tells me about the state of our relationship, so..."

"Tucker, I didn't mean no forever. It's just that..."

"Just that what? I thought we were headed somewhere. I thought we had a future."

"I did too. I mean, I do. It's just that I was engaged to someone else not that long ago, and it really did a number on my head."

"Are you comparing me to Peter?"

"Of course not! That whole engagement really took a lot out of me. I was enjoying us getting to know each other and taking our time. I just didn't expect for you to suddenly go down on one knee and propose. I was taken aback and scared."

"Look, Colleen, I love you. We fell hard and fast. I know what I want. I want my future to be with you, but I'm worried that you don't feel the same way. I never want to feel like I'm giving my heart to somebody and they just don't want it. I've had my share of broken hearts along the way."

"Tucker, nothing has changed for me. I want to be with you and build a life with you. I just need a little time. I want to make sure that this is the right thing for both of us. Can't we just take things a little slower?"

He smiled slightly. "You know, my mother always said I was a little bit impulsive. I guess I just thought if we love each other now, might as well make the jump to marriage but I didn't think about your feelings. I just thought I was doing this grand romantic gesture, and you hurt my pride when you said no."

She laughed. "I appreciate the gesture, and I really do hope you'll make it again one day."

"Well, if it's all the same to you, I think I'll wait a little while before I try that again."

Colleen reached across the table. "Forgive me?"

He smiled. "There's nothing to forgive. Now, I'm starving. I haven't had an appetite in days."

CHAPTER 5

Dawson stood in front of his house, his arms crossed. "Do you think we're ready?"

"Well, I reckon we're as close as we're going to get," Lucy said with a laugh. She had been right beside him the whole time, through every renovation and menu revision. She would never admit it, as stubborn as she was, but she had enjoyed watching the transformation of Dawson's home into The Inn At Seagrove.

He sometimes worried that her advanced age might cause her to retire when he decided to open the inn, but she'd jumped in head first right along with him.

"I sure hope we're ready. I've already got my first couple of reservations, and we open in two days."

"I know. And I'll be cooking ahead just so we have plenty of food. Pancakes are going to be a hit!"

Lucy had been very proud of creating a new recipe for caramel pecan pancakes with peach flavored maple syrup. She was chomping at the bit to serve it to the first visitors. The whole menu, in fact, was a sight to behold. Dawson hadn't seen Lucy this excited since Burt Reynolds came to visit the town two decades ago. She said looking at him made her feel things that she couldn't say in polite conversation.

"Oh, Dawson, it's beautiful!" Julie said as she walked up beside him and Lucy. She had driven up without him even noticing she was there, his attention completely devoted to looking at the landscaping he had just completed in the yard.

"You like it?"

"It's stunning! I love the pansies you planted over there. That violet color is just gorgeous and really makes the front of the house pop."

"I better get back inside before I burn those casseroles I put in the oven," Lucy said, rubbing Julie's arm before walking back in the house.

"Lucy got a snazzy new apron, I see," Julie said with a laugh.

"I'm not sure who's more excited, me or her," Dawson said. "I wasn't sure if I could get this place ready on time, but I think we're going to get there. My first guest is arriving day after tomorrow."

"I know you're so excited! I'm thrilled for you, Dawson," she said, grabbing his hand as they both stood there staring at the inn.

"I have you to thank for it."

Julie looked at him quizzically as he grabbed her other hand to face her. "Me? I haven't done anything."

"You've done a lot more than you realize. Encouraged me. Made me feel like I could really do this. And gave me the space to get it done without getting mad at me for not taking you out to fancy dinners. But, we're going to go to a fancy dinner to celebrate soon."

She smiled at him. "Dawson, if you'll remember, I had a husband who took me to a lot of fancy dinners for a lot of years and you see how that ended up. I would much prefer sitting in that swing over there with you, having an evening cup of coffee and listening to the waves roll in behind us. That's my celebration. And now every day gets to be a celebration."

"I think that might be the nicest thing anyone has ever said to me." He smiled as he leaned down and softly kissed her.

"It's true. I never thought this would be my dream life, but it is. I thought all my hopes and dreams were wrapped up in some big house in the city with a bunch of friends who weren't really my friends. But this place has become a part of my soul, and I can't imagine ever leaving here. So, you have my help for whatever you need because investing my time in this inn is investing my time in my forever home."

"Well, Julie Pike, I hope you mean that because I can't ever imagine losing you. I feel like my life didn't really start until we met. And since this place is like heaven to me, having you here just makes it even better."

"Better than heaven? Is that even possible?" she teased.

"I'm thinking it is," he said, leaning down to give her a longer kiss.

Suddenly, he heard someone clearing their throat. They broke apart, each of them turning around like two middle schoolers who had just been caught making out in the janitor's closet. Julie's daughter, Meg, stood there, her face red from embarrassment after catching her mom kissing Dawson. Some things never change. No kid wants to see their parent smooching on anybody.

"Oh, Meg, I didn't see you there..." Julie said, wiping her mouth with the back of her hand. Dawson did the same, the taste of her strawberry lip gloss clinging to his lips.

"I'm going to go inside and do some final touches on the kitchen cabinets. Good to see you, Meg," Dawson said, making a hasty retreat.

JULIE SAT at the picnic table, her daughter across from her, the ocean waves rolling gently to shore in the background. The sun was starting to set, a beautiful swath of pink wiping across the sky like God had painted it himself.

Meg seemed uneasy, almost embarrassed. She wasn't saying anything, so Julie decided she'd better break the ice.

"You look good. Have you been getting more rest?"

Meg finally looked up, shaking her head and smiling slightly. "I am so sorry, Mom."

Julie reached across the table and squeezed her hand. "You don't have anything to be sorry for. I'm the one who's sorry. I came on too strong, even though I was truly trying to help."

"I know. I guess I just wasn't ready to hear it. But you're right. You and Christian are both right. I don't know what's going on with me, but I need help."

Julie was glad to hear her say it, although she wished it wasn't true. "I'll do anything to help you. I hope you know that."

"It's just that I hated to ask. I didn't want to admit to myself or anyone else that I was struggling. And the last thing I wanted to do was disappoint you yet again."

Julie cocked her head. "Disappoint me? What on earth are you talking about?"

"I know that you were disappointed when I got pregnant, and I thought if I had the baby and turned out not to be a good mother, you would be disappointed all over again."

Julie's eyes welled with tears, and Meg's soon followed. "Honey, I've told you over and over that I've never been disappointed in you. And a lot of women go through this. It doesn't make you any less of a mother."

"Today, Dixie found me walking down the sidewalk. She took me into the bookstore and we had a little chat. She even gave me a book."

"Dixie is the wisest person I know," Julie said, chuckling.

"I wish she was my grandmother," Meg said under her breath. Julie slapped her hand playfully.

"Well don't ever let your real grandmother hear you say that."

"I called and made an appointment with my doctor tomorrow. I know you're busy with Dawson's opening, but I was hoping you might come with me?"

Julie smiled. She was so grateful Meg had asked her. "Of course, I will come with you. Dawson's place isn't opening for two days anyway, so tomorrow I will be right by your side."

"Thanks, Mom. Well, I better get back. I left Christian with the baby for a bit. I need to go get some more diapers before I head home." She stood up and walked around the table, hugging Julie's neck.

"We will get through this, Meg. Everything is going to be okay."

Meg smiled and nodded. "I believe you. I'll see you tomorrow. The appointment is at eleven o'clock."

"I'll meet you there."

As she watched her daughter walk toward her car, she was struck by what an adult she had become so quickly. Just a year ago, she was a college student with her eyes full of stars. Now, she was the mother of a baby girl who was counting on her. That was a lot of responsibility for a twenty year old, but Julie was determined to help her daughter make the most out of her life and Vivi's.

JULIE SAT beside her daughter as they waited for the doctor to come into the room. Because this wasn't really a medical check up, the nurse had taken them to the doctor's office so they could talk in private about what was going on with Meg.

"I don't know why I'm so nervous," Meg said, her leg bouncing up and down like a jittery jack rabbit.

"Everything is going to be fine," Julie said. She looked down at her granddaughter sleeping peacefully, something she loved to do during the daytime but not so much at night, and smiled. "Vivi is so beautiful. I mean, I might be biased, but I think she could be the most beautiful baby I've ever seen."

Meg chuckled. "Yes, I think you definitely might be biased." She peered over her mother's lap and looked at her daughter. "However, I would agree with you. Definitely the most beautiful."

Julie squeezed her hand. "I can't wait for her first Christmas. And then her first birthday. We're going to have so much fun spoiling her rotten!"

"It's hard for me to look forward to that right now."

"I know. But you will. The doctor will be able to help you."

As if on cue, a woman walked in wearing a white lab coat. She was pretty with long blonde hair and looked like she had just stepped out of a magazine. She smiled and reached out her hand.

"Hi, I'm Dr. Miller. You must be Meg?"

"Yes. And this is my mother, Julie Pike."

"Nice to meet you. I know you must've been expecting Dr. Hodges, but he's away on a trip right now."

Meg looked at her mother as if she was hesitant about talking to a new doctor. Julie squeezed her hand once again.

“Okay,” Meg said.

"I understand that you called and spoke to one of our nurses about having some issues with possible postpartum depression?"

"Yes. I mean, at least that's what I think I have. I just haven't been feeling myself since the baby was born."

The doctor smiled reassuringly. "Well, first let me say that this is a very common issue. We estimate that more than three million women experience this every single year after giving birth."

"Three million? Really?" Julie said.

"Yes. Like I said, we see this all the time. Thankfully, most cases are easily treatable by a doctor, and this normally resolves itself within a few months."

"A few months? That long?" Meg said.

Dr. Miller smiled again. "Well, to be honest, that's usually because the woman doesn't seek out any assistance. But you're here, and that's a good thing." She pulled out a chart. "There are three phases of the postpartum period after birth. The first phase is six to twelve hours after you give birth. It sounds like you did okay then?"

"Yes. I mean, I don't remember anything being wrong. I was just so focused on the baby."

"And then we have the two to six week period which we call the sub acute postpartum period."

"This all sounds very complicated," Meg said.

Julie looked at the doctor and raised her eyebrows, trying to give her a sign that Meg couldn't take in a whole lot of information right now.

"It sounds like you may have started having issues during that period of time?"

"I guess so. It really started a couple of weeks after Vivi was born. But now she's almost three months old."

"And now you're in the delayed postpartum period, which can last up to six months."

"Oh no," Meg said, her face falling a bit.

"Meg, this is very treatable. Coming to get help was a great first step to feeling better. So, let me ask you, are you experiencing insomnia? Loss of appetite? Irritability?"

"All of the above."

"What about problems bonding with the baby?"

Suddenly, without warning, Meg started to sob. It was like a huge amount of emotions were suddenly released right there in the doctor's office. Dr. Miller pulled a tissue from a box on her desk and handed it to Meg.

"Yes. I've had problems bonding. I feel so guilty," Meg said, blowing her nose into the tissue.

"No need to feel guilty. Meg, this has nothing to

do with your abilities as a mother. This is completely hormonal and very normal. We see it all the time."

"I don't want to miss this time with my daughter."

"Look, as far as your baby knows, you're her mother. You feed her, you comfort her, you talk to her. There will be no lasting effects."

Meg dried her eyes. Julie felt like she wanted to squeeze her daughter tight in that moment. She had no idea how Meg had even been holding it together this long.

"What kind of treatment are we looking at?" Julie asked.

"Well, we definitely recommend some counseling. There are some great new mother group sessions here at the hospital. But there are also individual counseling opportunities if you don't want to be in a group setting."

"I think I would like a group. I don't really have any friends here yet, so maybe that would help me."

"I think that would be good for you. The other thing we can try is some hormone therapy. Very simple stuff that you won't need long-term. Of course, there's also the option of doing an antidepressant, although there may be some side effects. And, honestly, some women can't tolerate those."

"I think I'd like to know more about the hormone therapy first."

Dr. Miller smiled. "Great. Let me go get you some informational flyers and some samples. I'll show you how to use the hormones, and then we'll set up an appointment to meet again in a couple of weeks."

As the doctor left the office, Julie could see a change in Meg's demeanor. The baby started fussing a bit, so Julie picked her up and held her close to her chest.

"That all sounds very promising," Julie said.

Meg nodded. "Yeah. I finally feel like there may be some light at the end of the tunnel."

Julie nodded and looked down at her granddaughter. "Vivi is such a blessing."

Meg leaned her head over onto her mother's shoulder. "Thanks for coming with me."

DIXIE TOOK another bite of her fried catfish. She hadn't eaten this much in years. Having someone who wanted to spend time with her and take her on real dates was new for her. When Johnny died, she gave up the idea of growing old with someone, but when she met Harry at one of her Parkinson's support group meetings, she felt a weird butterfly feeling in her stomach.

"How's your food, pretty lady?" Harry asked, winking at her across the table. They'd traveled two towns over to try out a new seafood restaurant right by the ocean. She loved hearing the seagulls squawking overhead, and the smell of sea air was always a welcome aroma. She never got tired of living by the ocean.

"It's scrumptious, doll," she said, winking back. They were sickening, even to her sometimes, but she loved it. No one would ever replace Johnny, but Harry was in a league all his own. A retired airline pilot and former Marine, he was a man's man, just like Johnny had been. He was also very handsome, with silver hair, broad shoulders and that rugged look one would've seen in an old cigarette ad. But he also had a heart of gold, and he treated her like she was his most prized possession.

"Tell me again why we had to travel almost half an hour away from Seagrove?"

She smiled. "My friends are a bit..."

"Nosy?"

"You could say that. They love me to pieces, but they worry. And the last thing I want is for them to be worried about me."

She thought back to how she'd told a little white lie to Julie and Janine the other day. Pretending she was dating multiple men had been a spur a the moment decision. It was better for them to think she was having the time of her life dating lots of fellas than know she was falling hard and fast for a man she'd met just a few weeks ago.

"Are you embarrassed of me?"

She waved her hand at him. "No! Of course not. I'm just not ready for them to meet you."

"I thought we were getting kind of serious, Dix," he said, a slight frown on his face.

She reached across the table and squeezed his hand. "Darlin', you're the first man who has ever captured my heart since Johnny died. This is all new to me. I haven't felt this way about another man in my life."

Harry also had a Parkinson's diagnosis, but his medications were working well at the moment. Still, he had plans to take Dixie on trips around the world while they both still had their health. They wanted to go to Ireland and Scotland to dig into Dixie's ancestry. They wanted to see Alaska together on a cruise. There were so many things to do while she still had life left in her and a new partner to enjoy things with again.

"I'll be as patient as you need me to be," he said, smiling at her.

Dixie's heart skipped a beat, and not because it was getting older and less efficient. Nope, this was love, and she was as scared as a cat in a room full of rocking chairs.

CHAPTER 6

Julie stood out on the deck Dawson had built and marveled at the scene in front of her. Residents from the island and the mainland had all come together to celebrate the opening of The Inn at Seagrove.

She was so proud as she watched Dawson work the crowd, going from person to person, shaking hands and giving hugs. The smile on his face warmed her heart. As he shook yet another hand, he smiled at her and waved from across the deck. She gave him a wink, letting him know it was okay that he was socializing while she sort of took a back seat, opting to stand near the dessert table to get the first crack at Lucy's peach cobbler when the time came.

"Great party, huh?" Janine said from behind her.

"It really is. Dawson hired a party planner from town, and I think she did a great job. Did you see the buffet?"

"Yes. I ate most of it," Janine said, shoving a stuffed mushroom in her mouth. As tiny as she was, William leaving had caused her to start eating a lot more food than Julie had ever seen her eat before. Julie swiped the last mushroom from Janine's hand and popped it in her own mouth. "Hey!"

"I'm hungry."

"Then go eat and stop lurking like some weirdo."

"I can't. I don't want to leave this peach cobbler."

Janine laughed. "Just take some now."

"It's rude. Everyone is still eating lunch. It's like cutting the wedding cake before the bride and groom get to the reception."

"Hey!" Colleen walked up with Tucker on her arm.

"Hey, you two. How's it going?" Janine asked.

"Just enjoying the party. This place looks amazing. Dawson has done a great job getting it ready."

"I know. I'm so proud of him. Did you see the renovated kitchen?"

"Yes. It's beautiful. And this deck is awesome. I mean, look at the view!"

"How are you, Tucker?" Julie asked.

He chuckled. "I'm fine, thanks. Don't worry. I won't propose to any of you and steal the focus of today's festivities."

"Tucker…" Colleen groaned. "He thinks these proposal jokes are funny, but they aren't!"

Tucker laughed. "Sorry, dear."

"We're going to go get some pasta salad. Want anything?" Colleen asked.

"Hey, see if they have more stuffed mushrooms," Janine said. Julie rolled her eyes.

As Colleen walked off, Julie looked at her sister. Her eyes were a million miles away, like she was searching for William in the crowd. He'd only been gone a few days, but she could tell Janine wasn't herself.

"Have you heard from him?"

Janine sighed. "No."

"Why don't you call him?"

"What's the use? I can't be in a serious relationship with someone in another state who may never come back to live here. We want different things."

"Seems to me you want each other," Julie said, taking a sip of her sweet tea.

"We do. But, I love it here. I finally found my home, and I don't want to leave. William doesn't feel the same way."

"I'm sorry, sis," Julie said. She didn't really have any answers for Janine. If Dawson left, she'd feel the same way.

"Thanks. Listen, I'm not really in a party mood. Can you tell Dawson that I'm so proud of him, but I need a little alone time?"

Julie rubbed her arm. "Of course. He'll understand. Call me if you need me."

Janine nodded as she walked toward the path home. Julie knew she'd find her sister snuggled up with a pint of ice cream by the time she got home later.

"Hey," she heard Dawson say from behind her. He slid his arms around her waist and kissed her neck. "I didn't expect this many people to show up. I hope we have enough food."

She turned around and smiled. "Don't worry. Lucy probably has food in the fridge that would be enough to feed all of these folks three meals a day for the next week."

Dawson laughed. "Yeah, she does kind of overcook, doesn't she?"

"So, when does your first guest arrive?"

"This evening at six. Kind of a late check-in, but at least we'll have everything cleaned up from the party by then."

"Any idea who the mystery guest is?"

"Lucy handled all of the reservations, actually. No idea who my first guest will be, but I'm excited to welcome him or her. They will be staying in Granny's room. We call it the Seagrove Suite. It has an attached bathroom and a nice sitting area."

"This is all so exciting," Julie said, beaming up at him.

"Thanks for being here."

"Where else would I be?"

"There's the man of the hour!" an older man said, slapping Dawson on the back. "Your grandmother would be grinning from ear to ear if she saw all this."

"Oh, hey, Dr. Carlson. How've you been?" Dawson said, turning his attention to the man.

Julie smiled and waved as she walked away, wanting to give him space to chat with his old friend. Of course, that meant walking away from the peach cobbler, which made her uncomfortable.

In the back of her mind, all she could really think about was her daughter, Meg. She'd opted not to come to the grand opening because she just wasn't feeling up to it. Still, she had hope that the new hormonal therapy and group counseling sessions would help Meg get back on her feet and enjoy being a new mother.

"Ain't this a great party?" Dixie said, walking up beside her, a glass of wine in her hand.

"Are you supposed to be drinking that with your medication?"

Dixie's head went back a bit, and she rolled her eyes. "Sugar, I'm like a hundred years old. I doubt a glass of wine every once in a while is gonna make much difference."

Julie laughed. "First of all, you're not that old. And secondly, I'm worried it might interact with your meds."

She waved her hand. "Nah, it's fine. I'm only having one glass because I'm a lightweight, and I just might dance on that table over there if I have another one."

"Then let's definitely keep it at one glass," Julie said, laughing. The mental image of Dixie on a table gyrating to the easy listening music playing at the DJ booth was a bit more than she could handle.

"I see Dawson's schmoozing it up pretty good. Maybe he should go into politics one day."

"Yuck. I doubt he'd ever want to do that."

"Probably true. He's done some great work here, hasn't he?"

"Yes. I'm really proud of him."

Dixie smiled. "I don't think I've ever seen two people so in love."

"What about you and Johnny?"

Dixie sighed. "Those were good times."

"Have you heard from William?"

"He called me this morning. Just told me he was settling in and got there safely."

"Janine's a wreck."

"I bet. I don't know what my son was thinking. Seagrove is his home, but he sure fights it. There's nothing wrong with living a small life and loving it, ya know?"

Julie smiled. "I know better than anyone. My so-called big life almost sucked my soul out of my body. Living here has turned me into the person I always wanted to be."

Dixie rubbed her arm. "Fate brought me the daughter I never thought I'd have."

"And it brought me the stand-in mother I always wanted."

Dixie chuckled. "Better not tell your momma you think that. She'd come down here and challenge me to a fight."

That was probably true. SuAnn definitely didn't like anyone taking the limelight away from her. She loved her mother, but having a nice, safe distance between them made for a much better relationship. The holidays would be coming soon, and she'd have to invite her, but she had plenty of time to prepare for that.

"Well, I'd better get on home and take my meds," Dixie said, handing the rest of her glass of wine to Julie. "Don't let this go to waste, ya hear?"

Julie laughed and nodded. "I'll be sure to finish it off before I dig into that peach cobbler in a minute."

As she watched Dixie walk toward her car, she looked around at all of the people on the deck and the beach and thought about this new life she'd built on Seagrove Island. Nothing could've prepared her for how her life had changed. Never in her wildest dreams had she thought of all of this, but God had blessed her in ways her mind couldn't have imagined a little over a year ago.

DAWSON WATCHED as everyone filtered off the property and back into their cars or golf carts. It had been a long day filled with fun and conversation, but he was ready to settle in for the night and meet his first guest when they arrived.

"I think everything went great," Julie said as she helped Dawson fold up the last of the tables.

"I think so too. I was surprised at how many people showed up."

They leaned the table against one of the many large oak trees. "Well, I wasn't. Everybody loves Dawson Lancaster, especially me." She put her arms around his waist and laid her cheek against his chest.

"I love you too," he said, pressing his lips to the top of her head. Her hair smelled like strawberries. She looked up and kissed him. Her breath smelled like peach cobbler. Dawson chuckled.

"What?"

"Exactly how much peach cobbler did you end up eating?"

Julie smiled slyly. "I plead the fifth."

"So, are you sticking around to meet my first guest?"

She stepped back and scrunched her nose. "Do you need me to? It's just that Janine didn't seem like herself when she left earlier, and I kind of want to get home and make sure she's okay. I also want to call and check on Meg..."

"No worries, Julie. You've been my rock today. Thank you so much for being here."

"Of course! I wouldn't have wanted to be anywhere else."

He gave her one last hug and kiss before watching her walk down the road toward home. Seagrove Island was the safest place on earth, as far as he was concerned, but he still watched her until he could see she was nearing the end of her driveway.

"I gathered up all of the tablecloths and put them in the wash. Room's ready for the first guest too."

"Thanks, Lucy," Dawson said, looking around the deck. "I'm going to take these tables to the storage barn, and then I'll be inside. If the guest arrives early, just let them know I'll be right there."

"Got it, boss," she said, with a laugh. Dawson knew Lucy was really the boss around there, and he was so thankful for her. Without his beloved Granny to keep him on the straight and narrow, Lucy had been a godsend to him. He couldn't imagine running the inn without her.

He walked down behind the house and put the tables into the barn. As he turned back, he saw a car pulling into the driveway. He'd also had some gravel brought in and spread on the side of the house to create a small parking area. It only held four cars, but it was enough for the inn.

By the time he walked through the back door and into the house, he could hear Lucy talking in the foyer.

This was it! His first guest and hopefully the beginning of a successful business. For some reason, he was a bit nervous, but he took a deep breath and pushed the swinging door from the kitchen, which led into the dining room.

For some reason, the voice sounded vaguely familiar to him. As he walked through the dining room and saw his first guest, he was stunned. Oh, this wasn't good.

"SuAnn?" he stammered as he stared at her. Looking unaffected, she forced a smile.

"Oh my. Aren't you Julie's... friend?" she said in her typical condescending tone.

"I'm her boyfriend, yes," he said. Lucy looked back and forth between them.

"Don't you think boyfriend sounds a little juvenile, dear?"

Dawson, took in a deep breath and counted to three in his head before speaking. "Welcome to The

Inn At Seagrove. Julie didn't tell me you were coming for a visit."

She chuckled. "She doesn't know I'm here. Please don't tell her. I plan to surprise her and Janine tomorrow."

"I... uh... I really don't think I can keep a secret like this from her..."

She furrowed her eyebrows. "Now, Dawson, you wouldn't want to ruin an old woman's long planned surprise for her daughters, would you?"

This woman was one of the most cunning he'd ever met, and he was certainly no match for her. What harm could it do to let her surprise Julie and Janine the next day? After all, he didn't want to call Julie and interrupt her evening with drama. Better to let her spend time with Janine and check on Meg without more problems.

"Fine. I'll keep your secret tonight, but you better let your daughters know that you're here tomorrow or I will."

SuAnn painted on a smile. "Thank you. And I'm very happy to see that you're so protective of my daughter. You know, she hasn't been on her own very much in her life. She needs someone watching out for her."

Dawson could feel his blood start boiling. He

pasted on a smile to match hers. "I can assure you that Julie doesn't need me to protect her. She's a very capable and smart woman, and I'm lucky to call her my girlfriend."

SuAnn made a grunting noise and then looked down at her suitcases. "I know this place isn't exactly a fancy hotel, but do you offer services to help me get these bags up to my room?"

He figured it probably wasn't the best move to attempt to strangle his first guest. "Of course. You're going to be in the Seagrove Suite, our best room. As our first official guest, we wanted to make sure that your stay here was as pleasant as possible."

"Well, that is certainly appreciated. I'll follow you."

He picked up her bags, wondering why she seemed to have brought everything she owned, and walked up the stairs. She followed behind him, saying nothing, which was probably a good thing because nothing that ever came out of her mouth seemed to be nice or appropriate.

He turned left down the hallway to the last room on the left. It overlooked the ocean and was bigger than the other rooms. In fact, it used to be two bedrooms, but years ago they had removed the wall to create a suite. Dawson had never moved into it, opting to keep the bedroom he had slept in as a child. It was the smallest one, but it held a lot of memories. He just couldn't think of turning that into a room to rent out, so even now he kept it for himself.

"Here we are." He opened the door and turned on the lights. He had to say that he was pretty proud of the decor. Julie had helped him pick out the colors and the bedding.

SuAnn walked in behind him, setting her overnight bag on the floor next to the vanity. She walked around the room slowly, saying nothing for a change. She peered out the window, touched the bedding and then turned around, with another fake smile on her face.

"Well, it's certainly very quaint. But, I think I'll enjoy the view."

Quaint. Code for small and not nearly fancy enough.

"I definitely think you will. Lucy is finishing up dinner right now, so if you're hungry, you're welcome to join us in the dining room."

"Actually, I think I will. I'm famished after such a long trip. Just let me freshen up and then I'll come down."

He nodded his head and closed the door behind

him before walking down the stairs. He had to admit, he had hoped she'd say no, opting to stay in her room for the night. But she didn't. In typical SuAnn fashion, she was going to insert herself into dinner and make everyone uncomfortable. And by everyone, he only meant himself and Lucy.

He walked into the kitchen and warned Lucy about what was to come. He even offered to let her eat dinner out on the deck so that she didn't have to endure spending time with Julie's mother. In a fleeting moment, he considered the fact that this woman might one day be his mother-in-law. That was pretty terrifying. But he loved Julie, and that meant he had to find a way to love her mother.

A few minutes later, as Lucy was setting the table, SuAnn appeared in the doorway. She had changed her clothes to a green cardigan sweater and a pair of black slacks.

"Well, hello there," Lucy said, reaching her hand out to shake SuAnn's.

"Hello. I'm SuAnn. And you are?"

"My name is Lucy."

"You're the cook here then?"

"Lucy is like a member of the family. She's my partner here at the inn," Dawson said, correcting her.

"Oh, dear, I hope I haven't said anything out of turn. I didn't mean any offense."

Of course she did.

"None taken," Lucy said, cutting her eyes at Dawson.

Dawson stood until both of the women had sat down. Even though it was their grand opening, their next guests would not arrive for a few more days, so he was stuck trying to figure out how to eat breakfast, lunch and dinner with a woman who definitely didn't like him and was more critical than anyone he'd ever met.

"I feel a bit overdressed," she said, looking at Dawson. "I just assumed we were dressing for dinner."

Dawson looked down at his T-shirt and jeans, suddenly feeling like he was naked at his own dining room table.

"So, what are we having tonight?" SuAnn asked.

"Well, we're having roast beef, oven roasted potatoes, caramelized carrots and for dessert, we'll be having my world famous peach cobbler." Lucy smiled broadly at Dawson.

"Sounds wonderful. Except for the peach cobbler. I'm not a fan."

Lucy stared at her, like she didn't understand her

language. "You're a southerner and you don't like peach cobbler?"

SuAnn nodded as she scooped potatoes onto her plate. "I guess I'm not your typical southerner."

"I guess not," Lucy mumbled under her breath. Dawson heard it, but if SuAnn heard it, she didn't act like it.

Dawson had never been so thankful for chewing. As long as he kept her chewing, she wasn't talking. He and Lucy talked about things that he'd done or needed to do around the property, and every time it seemed like SuAnn might get to say something, he passed her another dish of food, hoping she would just continue eating.

"I'm as full as a tick," she finally said. Dang. Now she was going to talk for sure.

"So, how was your trip here? Dawson tells me you're from the north Georgia mountains?"

SuAnn wiped her mouth and took another sip of sweet tea. "It's a long, boring drive. But, there wasn't nearly as much traffic as I had feared."

"Your husband decided to stay behind?" Dawson asked.

She looked down at her plate for a moment and then cleared her throat. He seemed to have touched a nerve. "He's got some issues with his legs. Long car rides are difficult for him."

"But wasn't he here at Christmas?"

She nodded slightly. "To be honest, I needed a little alone time. Marriage does that to people, you know."

He had a feeling there was more going on then she was letting on, but he decided not to poke the bear.

"Well, I'm sure you're tired from your long trip. Feel free to enjoy your room. You don't have to stay down here on our account."

She looked down at her watch. "But it's only seven-thirty. I'm old, but certainly not old enough to go to bed at this hour."

Great. She was planning on staying up and interacting with him. "I definitely wasn't saying that you're old. There's a TV in your room inside the armoire. We're connected to satellite, so we've got all kinds of channels."

"I don't really watch TV. I find it makes the mind kind of like mush. There's been lots of studies on that."

Dawson looked at Lucy like he was hoping she would have a better idea, but she ended up leaving him in the lurch. "Well, I better be getting in the kitchen. I have a lot of preparing to do for the week."

"Don't you need my help?" Dawson asked, hopefully.

Lucy stood up and walked toward the door to the kitchen. “No. You need to spend some time with your first guest. I wouldn't dream of intruding on that."

When she got on the other side of the kitchen door, she smiled slyly at Dawson out of view. He was going to get her back for this.

CHAPTER 7

Julie had been in a rush all day. She had stayed up late last night, talking to Janine and trying to encourage her to reach out to William. She hated to see her give up a relationship that had been so good for the both of them.

She also spent a good hour on the phone with Meg, encouraging her to keep believing that things were going to get better. She would start on her hormonal treatments that week, and she would have her first group counseling session soon. Julie felt confident that her daughter was going to get back on the right track soon.

After working most of the morning at the book-store, she had contacted Janine, Colleen and Meg and invited them to eat lunch with her on the square. They didn't get nearly enough time together, just chatting and spending time talking. That "girl time" was becoming more important to her as she got older.

Thankfully, they had all agreed. Most of the time, she met Dawson for lunch, but she was quite sure he was busy at the inn, interacting with his first guest. She hadn't had a chance to talk to him today, so she shot him at a quick text message telling him that she hoped everything was going well and that she would touch base with him that evening on her way home from work.

Dawson was good about letting her have time with her family and friends. He never tried to encroach upon that like Michael did. Michael had always hated when she had lunch dates with her friends, somehow thinking that meant that she didn't want to spend time with him. Now she didn't feel nearly as guilty as she used to about that.

"Glad you could make it," Julie said to Meg as she walked up, pushing the stroller with Vivi inside. Christian had to work, so Meg was on her own, which was another reason why Julie wanted to spend some time with her today.

"Me too. I think I needed to get out of the apartment for a while."

A few moments later Colleen and Janine made their way to the table from different sides of the square. Dixie was manning the bookstore or else Julie would've invited her too. She was so grateful for the strong female energy she had in her life now.

"Man, we've been slammed at the studio today," Janine said, as she sat down and leaned over to look into the stroller. "We had a new class this morning for women over sixty, and those ladies were rowdy!"

Julie laughed. "A rowdy yoga class? I'm not sure that's the way it's supposed to work."

"Things have been quiet at work for me today. Of course, I can't keep Tucker away from my desk. He's constantly leaving me a little love notes," Colleen swooned.

"Gag. Love notes cause situations like this to happen," Meg said, pointing at the baby and laughing.

Julie enjoyed the banter that she got to have with her adult daughters. It was a totally different kind of relationship than she'd had with them as kids. It was still taking some getting used to, especially the part about keeping her opinions to herself unless she was asked for her input. That was very difficult, especially when she saw her daughters making potential mistakes. But who was she to judge? She had certainly made her fair share of mistakes, even well into adulthood.

"What can I get you ladies?" Denitra asked. They all placed their typical orders, Janine getting her chicken salad pita, Colleen ordering soup and a sandwich, Meg getting a burger and fries, and Julie getting her favorite big salad. They rarely veered from what they got, although sometimes they would try something new. Once, Julie had gotten a new item on the menu called a seared tuna croissant. It was the most disgusting thing she'd ever eaten, and they quickly removed it from the menu after multiple complaints.

"I heard the bakery opened today. Has anyone tried it yet?"

"No, I haven't had a moment to take a breath today. I guess the holiday season tourists are starting to flock into town because the bookstore has been crazy busy this week," Julie said, taking a sip of her water.

"I love the name," Colleen said. For a long time, the bakery did not have a sign up, but one had finally been erected the day before. It was called Hotcakes.

"We will have to check it out. I'm hoping they have poundcake."

"Maybe we can run in there before we all have to go back to work," Colleen said.

"Some of us don't go back to work," Meg corrected.

"You know what I mean."

"Actually, taking care of a baby is definitely considered work," Julie said. "It's harder than anything I have to do at the bookstore."

"Very true. I mean, I'm not a mother, but I know you're working hard, Meg. And being sleep deprived doesn't help." Janine said.

A few minutes later, Denitra brought their food and they ate and chatted for over half an hour. As they settled up on the bill and left a tip on the table, Julie looked up at the bakery one more time.

"Do y'all have time to go check out Hotcakes?"

They all looked at each other and then started laughing. "I think it's pretty safe to say that we are a bunch of sugar addicts, so we might as well admit it and see what kind of decadent desserts we can find," Janine said.

They all stood up and walked down a few storefronts before making their way to the bakery. There had been a line all morning, but thankfully it was pretty light at the moment, probably because most people were at lunch.

"Let's do this," Julie said, pushing the door open and then holding it for Meg to get the stroller through.

The place was really cute inside, a southern theme definitely on display. There were lots of whites and pinks and a little bit of gold here and there. The tables had beautiful white lace tablecloths while the walls were a mixture of white and pink stripes. There were big mirrors with painted white wrought iron all over the walls, as well as some ornate gold candle wall sconces. Most striking were the older, black-and-white pictures displayed on the walls.

"These look familiar," Janine said as she looked at one of the photos on the walls.

Julie walked closer. "Yeah. I can't place where I've seen these before..."

"Well, you should recognize that woman. She's your great grandmother!"

Julie froze in place, staring at the picture. Who just said that? It couldn't be. It was impossible. She had to be imagining things.

But no. She turned around slowly to see her mother standing there, her hair pulled up in a bun, wearing a hand embroidered apron that she knew for a fact belonged to her grandmother.

"Mother, what on earth are you doing here? You got a job at the bakery?" Janine asked, her eyes wide.

SuAnn laughed and waved her hand in the air. "Of course not. I own the place!"

Meg, Colleen, Janine and Julie all just stood there, staring like they were looking at an alien. SuAnn had a big grin on her face, obviously waiting for them to be excited. Excitement wasn't one of the words Julie would use to describe the scene.

"Grandma, you bought a bakery?" Colleen stammered.

"I didn't buy a bakery, sweetheart. I made one. I rented the space and created my own business!"

"Wait. Does that mean... You're living here now?" Janine said, the words slowly coming out of her mouth one at a time, as if each one was getting stuck on her lips.

"Of course it does. I couldn't very well live hours away and run this bakery every day."

"But... Why didn't you tell us..." Julie said. She couldn't seem to formulate actual sentences.

Just then, more customers came through the door, and SuAnn seemed to be the only person working. It would be just like her mother to think she could do everything and not hire any employees.

"Hold that thought! I've got some more paying customers coming in," SuAnn said, trotting back over behind the counter. "Welcome to Hotcakes!"

The four women moved over against the wall and huddled up like they were in a football game.

"I can't believe this. I really, truly can't believe this. What on earth is happening?" Julie said, mumbling in a monotone voice like she was losing her mind.

"What about Buddy? " Meg asked.

"I don't know, honey, but your grandmother is up to something for sure. She doesn't even like to work, much less run her own business. I don't know why she's here."

"Oh Lord. You don't think she wants to live with us, do you?" Janine asked, biting her fingernails.

"Well she can't live with me. My apartment is too small," Meg said, obviously trying to take herself out of the running.

"Well there's no room at the house," Colleen said.

"Sorry about that. Business has been booming today!" SuAnn said, once the store had cleared out again.

Julie sucked in a deep breath and blew it out

slowly, determined to get some information this time. "Mom, why in the world did you do this without telling any of us?"

SuAnn sat down in one of the chairs, propping her feet up on the one across from her. "Because if I told you, I knew you'd try to talk me out of it. But, I needed a new start."

"What do you mean by a new start?" Julie asked, slowly sitting down in another chair.

"Well, you see, I'm not getting any younger. I wanted something fun and exciting, and this place wasn't so bad when I visited over Christmas. So, I decided what better place to open my own bakery and sell your grandmother's pound cake? I mean, we sell other things also. Everything except that nasty peach cobbler. Yuck."

"But, you could've opened a bakery up in the mountains where you live. Where your husband lives also..." Janine said.

"He's not my husband anymore," she said, looking down at her hands resting on her lap.

"What?" Julie said, her mouth hanging open. If there was one thing she knew about Buddy, it was that he worshiped her mother. Or at least that's the way it seemed from the outside.

"Buddy was too... boring... for me. He never

wanted to do anything fun. The man hardly ever spoke."

"And yet you stayed married to him for many years," Colleen interjected.

"I know, right? I wasted so many years of my time. But the truth is, my whole family is here. I never get to see you girls, and now there's a new baby."

"Thanks a lot, Meg," Colleen murmured in her sister's ear.

"Shut up," Meg whispered back.

"I wanted to be with my family. I'm not getting any younger, and these are my golden years. All of my friends have their families around, and my family just ran off to some godforsaken little coastal town. This might not be my cup of tea, but I moved here so I could make the best of it."

"So you actually moved? Like, you have a house or an apartment?" Julie said.

"Well, not exactly. I was so busy worrying about getting this place open that I didn't have a chance to look for a place to live. And, I don't have a whole lot of money yet, so I can't really invest in a house..."

Julie's stomach churned. *Please don't ask to live with me. Please don't ask to live with me.*

"So where have you been staying?" Janine asked.

"Well, I actually just got here yesterday."

"You just got here yesterday, and you opened today? But you don't even have employees here to help you."

"I did. I do, actually. Young girl that has been helping me get things set up behind the scenes. But she wasn't available today."

"Your only employee wasn't available on your opening day?" Colleen said.

"Well, she might have quit. But that's neither here nor there. I'll find somebody to help out."

"Back to my original question. Where did you stay last night? In your car?" Janine asked.

SuAnn smiled, but not in a normal way. She smiled and that sly way she always did when she was up to no good. "Well, there's this wonderful little inn that I found out about..."

"No. No you did not. You did not stay at the inn. The doors just opened. You did not take up space as his first guest ever." Julie said.

"Oh, but I did."

"WHY DIDN'T you call me last night? I can't believe you didn't tell me she was in town!" Julie said as

Dawson stood there trying to defend himself. She had been hammering on for more than five minutes, not giving him the ability to even say a word.

"Julie, she asked me not to ruin the surprise. I assumed she was trying to just surprise her two daughters. She laid on a pretty big guilt trip."

Julie sat down at one of the picnic tables on the deck and stared out over the vast ocean. Normally she found this place to be very peaceful, but right now she kind of wanted to run straight out into the water and see what would happen.

"Well, she certainly succeeded in surprising us."

He sat down across from her. "I'm really sorry I didn't tell you. I thought I was doing a nice thing for your mother."

"I just cannot believe she's here, and for good. I never would've predicted that she would've left her husband and moved here without telling anyone." Julie put her head in her hands.

"I know this isn't an ideal situation..."

"Ideal? This is horrible, Dawson. My mother, and I love her, is like some sort of poisonous octopus with these tentacles that just curl around you and cut your very air supply off."

"Is it possible you might be just a little overdramatic right now?" Dawson said, shrinking down a bit as if he was afraid she was going to slug him.

She sighed and laid her head on the table. "It's just that I love my life here. I love you. I love Dixie. I love the bookstore. And even though I love my mother, she just sucks the life out of me sometimes. This is the most drama free place I've ever lived, but that's all about to change."

"Maybe not. Maybe she really did come here because she misses her family, and I don't think you would ever forgive yourself if your mother died and she didn't get to spend time with all of you."

She sat up and glared at him, her eyes squinting. "Did she tell you to say that? Has she gotten to you? That sounds like something she'd say."

Dawson laughed. "Yes, last night we had several brainwashing sessions where she told me what to say."

"Very funny. I don't know what to do."

"What can you do? Burn down her bakery?"

"You probably shouldn't give me any ideas right now because I have a lighter, and I can get an alibi," Julie said, laying her head back down on the table.

"Look, there's nothing your mother can do that is going to break us apart. There's nothing she can do to make you lose your business or your friendships or your relationships with your daughters."

"You underestimate her."

"Maybe this is a chance for you to build a new relationship with her. Set boundaries. You're a grown woman. You have the right to tell her what's acceptable and what's not acceptable."

She looked at him. "Bless your heart. That all sounds very logical. But, this is my mother, and you can't use logic when it comes to her. I'm telling you she will cause trouble one way or the other, and waiting to figure out how she's going to do it is like sitting on a grenade waiting for it to explode."

"Okay, I didn't need that visual."

Julie finally laughed. "Please just promise me you'll protect yourself. I'm going to encourage her to find another place to live as soon as possible, but I hope you won't let her get in your head. She's very good at that."

"I promise. I'll be on guard."

"I mean, maybe it would be better if I had her come sleep on my sofa."

Dawson reached across the table and took her hands. "You have enough on your plate. I'm a grown man, and I can handle your mother. And who knows, one day she might be my mother-in-law."

Julie stared at him, her eyes wide. That was the first time she'd heard him mention anything about ever getting married, and honestly she hadn't thought about it much herself. Her marriage to Michael had been quite enough for one lifetime, but maybe Dawson was thinking differently than she was.

"What?"

"Okay, so by that deer in the headlights look, I'm going to take it that you're not ready to talk about marriage. Let's just forget I said that, put it in a box and move on."

She smiled. "I think my brain is just a little overloaded right now."

He stood up and pulled her up with him, bringing her into a tight hug. "We will get through this together. Maybe your mother being here is going to be some kind of blessing in disguise."

"You're so cute. And so, so naïve."

CHAPTER 8

Meg sat in the uncomfortable plastic chair and waited for the meeting to start. The counselor seemed nice enough. She was probably around her mother's age, so not overly easy for her to relate to personally, but she said she had six children and went through postpartum depression with four of them. The thought alone made Meg never want to have another child again.

Postpartum depression was no joke.

There were days when she felt like she was just about to pop her head out from under the dark swamp waters she was in, but then she'd get pulled right back down again. The doctor had adjusted her hormones last week, and at first it seemed to help a little. But, then she found herself crying in the bathtub for over an hour while Christian rocked Vivi to sleep one night.

Five other women milled into the room and found seats, no one really looking at each other yet. PPD really didn't make women overly social. They were probably just like her, doing the best they could to just stay upright.

"Welcome to the Thursday morning PPD support meeting. I'm your host and head counselor, Tammy Akins. I'm a lifelong resident of the Charleston area, and the mother of six crazy kids, ages ranging anywhere from four to fourteen..."

"Dear God in heaven. Who has that many kids nowadays?" the woman beside her whispered. Meg couldn't help but giggle, causing Tammy to look at her for a moment before continuing her welcome message.

"Before we get started, why don't we go around and introduce ourselves. Tell us about your baby, your family situation and how you're struggling..."

"God, I hate introducing myself," the woman whispered. Meg looked at her and nodded.

"Me too."

"Why don't we start with you, ma'am," Tammy said, pointing at Meg.

"Me?"

"Yes, hon, you."

Ugh. "Well, my name is Meg. I'm twenty years old, boyfriend, three month old baby girl named Vivi."

"And how're you struggling, hon?"

Meg took in a deep breath and blew it out. "A lot of crying, depression, no motivation. And sometimes I don't feel… connected… to my baby. Or my boyfriend."

"That must be hard," Tammy said.

"Duh," the woman beside her whispered.

"Pardon?" Tammy said to the woman beside Meg.

"Oh, nothing," she said, faking a smile and waving her hand. Meg really liked this chick, whoever she was.

"Have you talked to your doctor?"

"Yes. She has me on some hormone stuff, but I don't think it's working. Next stop is medication."

Tammy nodded and smiled. "Well, there's no shame in taking medication if you need it. Now, let's move to you." She pointed at the woman beside Meg.

The woman sighed, like she was being put out to be there in the first place. "Okay, well, I'm Darcy. Twenty-three years old. Married. Four month old baby boy named Hatcher."

"And your struggles?"

"Well, my main struggle seems to be judgmental people who think there's something wrong with a woman having emotions after the birth of a baby."

"Excuse me?"

"My mother and husband basically forced me to come to this meeting because they say my personality has changed since becoming a mother. Oh, I'm sorry, but I went from being up all night dancing and having a good time with friends to being up all night wiping poop off a baby's butt and putting cream on my cracked nipples. Pardon me for taking some time to grieve my old life and learn the ropes of my new one."

Everyone sat in stunned silence. For the first time, Meg felt like someone just spoke exactly what she was feeling.

"You know, everyone focuses on the baby once its born, but nobody seems to really give the mother some grace and some space. We're automatically labeled crazy or depressed, when maybe we just need some time to adjust. Maybe we aren't meant to be the same person we were before."

Tammy smiled. "You've given this a lot of thought."

"Well, I've had a lot of time on my hands, what with being up all night long crying and so forth."

Again, the room fell silent. Awkward didn't even begin to cover it.

"Okay, then, why don't we continue going around the room..." Tammy said, diverting her attention away from Darcy.

When the meeting was finally over an hour later, most of the women went straight to their cars. Meg walked over to the snack table and wrapped the last doughnut in a napkin, dropping it into her large tote bag before turning toward the door.

"Well, that was a total waste of time," Darcy said from behind her.

"You think so?"

Darcy wasn't what one would describe as a typical looking mother. She wore black, ripped jeans, a white band tee and high top white sneakers that looked like they stepped right out of the 90's. She looked more like an angry teenager than a new mom.

"Did you get any useful information out of that whine session?"

Meg shrugged her shoulders. "I mean, it feels good to know other women know how I'm feeling. It made me feel less alone, I guess."

"Well, all it did was make me want to remove my ears and throw them in the ocean." She walked past

Meg and toward the door, grabbing the last cupcake on the table.

"Hey?" Meg called to her.

"Yeah?"

"Do you like pound cake?"

"Wow, this place looks like Gone With The Wind threw up," Darcy said as they walked into Hotcakes. Meg didn't know why she'd chosen to bring her new acquaintance into her grandmother's bakery, but it was too late to go back now.

"My grandmother just opened this place."

"Oh. Sorry," Darcy said, softly.

"It is a little bit… much… but we're younger so maybe we just have better taste," Meg said, with a laugh.

"Yeah."

"There's my darlin' granddaughter!" SuAnn said, running out from behind the counter and hugging Meg. She normally wasn't this touchy feely, but her grandmother would do anything for the benefit of the crowd watching her. And right now she had a whole bakery full of people who needed to believe she was a doting grandmother full of love and cuddles.

"Hey, Grandma," Meg said. "This is my new friend, Darcy."

SuAnn eyed her carefully, looking her up and down. Meg knew she was internally criticizing Darcy's attire, but she hoped her grandmother would keep her mouth shut, for once.

"Nice to meet you, Darcy," SuAnn said, shaking her hand and then wiping it on her apron like Darcy had a communicable disease or something.

"You too. Nice little place you have here."

"Thank you. Have you been to a bakery before, dear?"

Darcy looked at Meg quizzically and then back at SuAnn. "Hasn't everyone?"

Meg cleared her throat. "Grandma, could we get a couple of pieces of poundcake?"

SuAnn looked at Darcy for a moment longer than necessary. "Of course. Let me get that for you. Just find a table."

Meg led Darcy over to a table, and they sat down.

"Boy, she's something else," Darcy said.

"Yeah, you could say that."

"So, are you planning to go back to those meetings?"

"Aren't you?"

Darcy sighed. "I don't know. My mother and husband are going to drive me batty if I don't, but it just wasn't my jam, ya know?"

SuAnn walked to the table and set two pieces of poundcake in front of them, shooting a smile at Darcy. "Enjoy, ladies."

"Thanks, Grandma."

As Meg watched her grandmother walk back behind the counter, she second guessed her choice to go there. SuAnn had an uncontrollable mouth and absolutely no filter between her brain and her lips.

"So, are you from around here?" Meg asked.

"Nah. We just moved here from NYC, actually."

"How in the world did you end up in Seagrove?"

"Long story, but basically my husband got transferred with his concrete paving company. And now, here we are, right in the heart of podunkville. No offense."

"None taken. I'm not from here originally, either. I grew up in Atlanta."

"And how did you end up here?"

"Parents divorced, mother moved here. I was in Paris at university. Got pregnant at nineteen, came home and kept the secret. You know, the typical story," Meg said with a laugh.

"Wow. You've got a great backstory compared to mine. All I did was get married and have a kid."

Meg took another bite of poundcake. "Well, we have one thing in common, I guess."

"PPD?"

"Yep."

Darcy sighed. "I guess I'm going to have to go back to the meetings."

Meg nodded. "Probably a good idea. But, at least we found each other. I don't have any friends in town."

"Me either," Darcy said, smiling slightly. "I guess I do now."

JANINE PICKED AT HER SANDWICH. Today hadn't been the best. William had been gone for two weeks now, and she missed him all day, every day. Her hand had lingered over the keypad on her phone so many times as she thought about whether she should text him or not. But, her pride reeled her back in each and every time.

Her class schedule had been grueling today, with students showing up at seven in the morning and classes ending at five. She was so thankful for the business, but what was she doing it for, really?

When she'd opened the studio, her grand plans had included William, a couple of dogs and a white picket fence. Part of her had even allowed herself to hope for children, although adoption would be their only option at her age. She'd been so excited thinking about the prospect of being a mother one day, hopefully through the foster care system. Now, everything had fallen apart right in front of her face, and she didn't know what to do to get her motivation back.

"Well, if it isn't my oldest daughter," SuAnn said, loudly of course, as she took the seat across from Janine. All hopes for a nice, quiet lunch were dashed.

"Hi, Mom." She stirred her cream of chicken soup for the hundredth time, still without taking a bite.

"You're looking a little glum today, dear. Wrinkles are a very real thing, and they come on much faster if you frown."

Janine wanted to run out into traffic, only there wasn't any in the small town. "Mother, please. I can only take so much today."

"Is this about that William fellow?"

"I'm not talking about this with you."

"So, it is about him. Well, if you want to know what I think..."

"I truly don't."

"I think you need to call him up, apologize for breaking up with him and get on the next plane to Texas."

Janine stared at her. "What?"

"Dear, and forgive me for pointing out the obvious, you're not getting any younger. As you get older, there aren't very many good men to choose from. Letting a perfectly good one go isn't wise."

Janine considered throwing her bowl of soup at her own mother for a moment, but thought better of it. Who would ever come to her studio again to learn about peace and tranquility if she nutted out at the local bistro?

"Do you ever think about what you're saying?"

"I know it's not popular to think this way in this day and age, but a good man is worth his weight in gold. Don't you want to settle down? You're exhausting to keep up with, Janine."

Janine glared at her mother. "I don't even understand what you're talking about. I'm literally sitting right here in front of you, stable as can be with my own business. You're the one telling me to go running off to some other state chasing after a man."

"It just breaks my heart to see you all alone."

"I'm not alone, Mother. I'm an independent woman who has her family all around her."

"Yes, but your family won't snuggle up with you at night. And your family isn't going to grow old with you, sitting on the front porch watching your grandchildren play in the front yard. You keep this up and you're going to be one of those old women at the nursing home all by herself."

Janine couldn't believe what she was hearing, although it shouldn't have come as any surprise given the history she had with her mother. "I need to get back to work. I have a class in fifteen minutes, and I've lost my appetite."

Janine stood up and started walking towards the studio. "I don't know why you girls get mad at me so easily!" her mother yelled to her as she walked away.

"I don't know. I guess it will remain a mystery," Janine yelled back, rolling her eyes.

DAWSON SAT at the edge of the dock, his fishing pole dangling in the water. This was the first break he'd had in the last couple of weeks. New guests had come and gone, all of them leaving rave reviews, which made him feel a lot better about taking the risk on opening the inn.

But, living with Julie's mother had been worse than anticipated. She stuck her nose in everybody's business, even those very same guests. She rarely stayed in her room, unless it was late at night, and even then he had caught her in the living room poking through his grandmother's antiques once or twice.

She claimed she had insomnia and that she was bored. He wanted to invite her to go on an adventure outside of his house, but he didn't think it was a very nice thing to say.

Thankfully, she was still at work at the bakery since she couldn't keep an employee. In the two weeks that she had been open, the two teenagers she'd hired had already quit. Apparently, she wasn't the easiest boss to work for.

"Hey, Dawson," Colleen said, walking up behind him.

"Oh, hey. What can I help you with?"

"I just wanted to stop by and drop off this guest list. Mom said you're going to be hosting the Halloween masquerade ball here. That's very exciting."

"Yeah, it's a big undertaking, but I think it will be

good for business." He took the paper from Colleen's hand.

"I think they got about twenty people to sign up," Colleen said. Julie and Dixie had been nice enough to post a sign-up list at the bookstore so that people around town could register to come to the event. It was free, but they would also be selling raffle tickets and having a silent auction.

"That's great. Care to join me in a little fishing?"

Colleen laughed. "Not really my thing, but I don't mind sitting with you for a bit. I don't wanna interrupt if you're trying to get some peace from my grandmother."

Dawson laughed. "My lips are sealed. But you definitely are welcome to sit down."

Colleen sat down beside him, her legs dangling over the water. He enjoyed being around Julie's daughters. Although they were adults, they were always respectful and nice and welcomed him. That had been one of his concerns when he first met Julie. Would her daughters accept him or be upset that their mother wasn't with their father anymore?

Thankfully, they had accepted him with open arms. Of course, Julie's ex, Michael, had been the one to screw their marriage up anyway.

"So, how is my grandmother doing here?"

Dawson smiled. "She is… interesting."

"That's one way to put it," Colleen said, giggling. "Look, you don't have to mince words with me. I know how she is."

"I don't know how Julie and Janine grew up with her. Nothing is ever good enough. And she's got this way of pretending she's giving you a compliment but it's really a put down. It's kind of like walking through a field full of land mines."

"I am so sorry. We're trying to figure out how to get her an apartment or something, but the bakery isn't bringing in enough money yet and she doesn't seem to have any money of her own. I don't really understand that. "

"Has anyone asked her about that?"

Colleen smiled. "I don't think anybody wants to really pull at that string."

"I totally understand."

Suddenly, the peace was broken. "Well, hello, my granddaughter. I didn't expect to see you here."

Colleen cut her eyes at Dawson before they both turned around.

"Hi, Grandma. I was just dropping by to give Dawson a guest list for the masquerade ball."

"Sounds fancy. I'll be looking forward to that."

“That's still a couple of weeks away. Don't you think you might be in your own place by then?"

SuAnn pulled out a chair from one of the tables and sat down. She waved her hand at Colleen. "There's no hurry. Besides, I'm sure Dawson appreciates me helping to pay his bills around here."

Dawson turned back to the water, his jaw clenching. “Grandma, you shouldn't say things like that."

"No, it's okay,” Dawson said, reeling in his fishing line. "Speaking of my bills, I need to make a quick phone call to the mortgage company. I had a question about our taxes. You ladies enjoy your talk," Dawson said, jumping up as quickly as he could.

As he walked away, Colleen stared at him, a sly smile on her face. He had now joined Lucy in the ranks of stranding someone else with SuAnn.

CHAPTER 9

Colleen couldn't get away fast enough. Dawson was savvy, she'd give him that. Her grandmother had reeled her in, patting the table across from where she was sitting.

"You're not going to run off right now, are you?"

"Grandma, I actually have a date with Tucker tonight."

SuAnn looked down at her watch. "It's not late enough for a date yet. Have a seat. Talk to your old grandma for a few minutes."

"Okay," Colleen said, begrudgingly. It wasn't that she didn't love her grandmother, but she didn't relate to her at all. Julie had not been the kind of mother that SuAnn was. She had always been encouraging, rarely critical, probably because she had grown up the way she did.

"So, tell me about this Tucker."

"Well, he's a toy inventor. We work for the same company now. He's a wonderful person." Giving her grandmother as little information as possible was always the best route.

"And?"

"And what?"

"Do you see yourself settling down with this boy?"

"Well, first of all, he's a man, Grandma. And second of all, he proposed recently but I said no." SuAnn's eyes bugged out of her head.

"You said no? Colleen, you should never say no when a man proposes. He may never ask again."

Colleen laughed. "I love him, and I think we'll get married one day. But, I'm not ready."

SuAnn shook her head and clicked her tongue. "Dear, you need to rethink that. If this boy has a nice job and is good to you, you need to grab him while you can. There are so many single women out there. Lots of competition. You're never going to find the perfect one, so what's the sense in waiting?"

"Didn't you just leave your husband? You should understand better than anyone that you don't get married until it's the right person and the right time."

"You said you think he's the right person. What difference does it make if it's next month or ten years from now?"

"Because I'm not ready. And that's that. Look, I've got to get going. I don't want to keep Tucker waiting."

"I think you're keeping Tucker waiting right now," SuAnn called to her as she walked away. "You need to strike while the iron is hot!"

Colleen laughed as she made her way back to her car. Her grandmother really was something.

MEG WALKED DOWN THE SIDEWALK, looking at her phone. Christian was having trouble getting the baby to sleep, and she was on her way to her group session.

She and Darcy had become fast friends, although they had very different personalities. But she loved the fact that Darcy spoke her mind. It reminded her a little bit of her grandmother, but she found it endearing on Darcy. Not so much with her grandmother.

"Hey, there, Meg!" Dixie said. She was standing outside of the bookstore, lining up some books on a little metal shelf that they kept outside when the weather was good.

"Hey. How's business today?"

"Pretty good. Why don't you come on in. We got some new mango peach tea I wanted you to try."

"Sure. I have about ten minutes before my meeting anyway."

The two women walked inside, and Dixie poured her a glass of tea. They sat down at the table with Dixie telling the only other customer in the store to come get her if she needed any help.

"Boy, I've got to get off my feet today. One of the side effects of my Parkinson's medications is that it gives me fluid around my ankles if I'm on my feet too much." She put her feet up on the chair across from her.

"How are you feeling?"

"Good. I'm still alive and kicking, and as long as I wake up on this side of the ground, I think I'm doing good."

Meg laughed. She loved being around Dixie with her energetic personality. It gave her hope that she could grow old and be happy like Dixie was.

"So, I guess you saw that my grandmother is the owner of the bakery?"

"Yes, I've heard. I haven't seen her yet, although she's not a real big fan of mine."

"Well, that's because she's jealous. She doesn't like that you have such a great relationship with Mom. She is sort of a competitive type."

Dixie laughed. "Well nobody can take away somebody's mother. I'm just your mother's friend."

"My mother thinks of you more like a mother than her own, but we won't say that to my grandmother."

Dixie laughed. "Yes, let's not say that. "

"Grandma can be very difficult. I ran into her yesterday and she told me to stop going to group counseling meetings because I didn't need to be airing my dirty laundry in public."

Dixie looked stunned. "She said that?"

"She did."

"Well, I hope you're not going to listen to her. You need to do what's right for you."

Meg smiled gratefully. "Thank you. And this tea is amazing!"

"It is good, isn't it." Dixie smiled at her. "You know, you have much more light in your eyes today than I've seen in a while."

"I'm feeling better. The doctor adjusted my hormones, and I have to say those meetings are actually helping me. I met a new friend, and I'm starting to feel like my old self again."

Dixie reached across the table and squeezed her hand. "And it will only get better from here."

WILLIAM SAT AT HIS DESK, staring out the window over the city. He was thankful to at least have a park near his office building, although it was nothing like looking out over the ocean or being able to walk down to the marsh anytime he wanted.

He missed Seagrove more than he would've thought. But, mostly, he just missed Janine. Her laugh. The sweet smell of her thick, curly hair. Her snarky comments and goofy jokes.

So many times, he had typed her number into his phone, intending to call her and tell her how much he missed her. But what good would that do? She had already said she didn't want a long distance relationship, and really how would that ever work anyway?

He felt like calling her might just be prolonging

the inevitable. Still, he really wanted to hear her voice and know that she was okay.

He usually talked to his mother a few times a week, and so far he had refrained from asking much about Janine. What if she was starting to date other people? What if she hated him? These were things he just preferred not to know.

Going home to an empty apartment every night was getting kind of depressing, even after only a few weeks. He knew that he needed to get on with his life and build something new, but it was hard.

He hadn't expected to miss that little island so much. But, there were no big opportunities there, and he had to go in the direction that would allow him to build his career. If there was one thing his father had instilled in him at a young age, it was that a man needed to work hard and be strong.

Right now, he wasn't feeling very strong.

"You're here late." He looked up to see his boss, Tina, standing in the doorway. She was tough as nails, and at first they had butted heads quite a bit. But now they had become pretty good friends, at least from his perspective.

"I'm the new guy. Have to impress the boss," he said, laughing. Tina was a VP of the company, and she'd been assigned to oversee him as he started the new division.

She walked closer and sat down in the chair across from his desk. "You've already done that. Our numbers are on an upward swing."

"We are a new branch. There's nowhere to go but up."

"I mean they are exceeding all expectations. You should be proud of yourself for what you've done in such a short period of time."

"Well, I'm glad you think so. I really want to make this place successful."

She squinted her eyes. "You seem a little down today? Is everything all right?"

He shrugged his shoulders. "Just thinking about everybody back home. This was such a quick move, I really didn't have a chance to wrap things up there like I wanted."

She nodded. "I understand. When I left Los Angeles, it was quite a culture shock to come here. But, I like it. And I know you will adjust also. Remember, I've only been here a couple of weeks longer than you have. I'm still learning the ropes too."

"I'm sure everything will be okay for both of us. Are you headed out for the evening?"

She laughed. "Actually, I think I'm going down to Malone's to get a nice big glass of wine and watch some sports."

He leaned back in his chair. "You watch sports?"

"Oh yeah. I grew up with three brothers, so I definitely enjoy pretty much any sport."

William was surprised to hear that given how she looked. She was tall, long legs and bleached blonde hair. A couple of the guys in the office spent most of the day ogling her since she looked like a Barbie doll had just sprung to life. He'd pulled the men aside and told them staring at the big boss wasn't okay and certainly wasn't the right career move.

"Well, you enjoy your wine, and I'll see you here at the morning meeting." He looked down at his files, trying to decide which one to finish before going back to his sparse new apartment.

Tina stood and sat on the edge of his desk. "You know, life is about more than working."

"Not for everyone," he said, with a sigh.

"Why don't you join me?"

"What?"

"Come to Malone's with me. Have a beer or a glass of wine, relax for the evening. You're going to burn yourself out."

"To clarify, are you asking as a coworker or are you asking me on a date?"

She smiled, batting those long, most likely fake, eyelashes. "Well, if it makes you more comfortable to think of this as some kind of business meeting, then we'll go with that."

"I don't think you really answered the question."

Tina stood up, laughing as she sauntered over to the door. "I'll meet you downstairs in ten minutes."

As William watched her walk down the hall, he wondered what he was getting himself into. Maybe he should just stay at his desk and then go home and eat another slice of cold pizza. Or, maybe he needed to try to embrace this new life he'd chosen.

JULIE PUSHED OPEN the door of the bakery and stomped inside, her mission spurring her feet to move faster than normal. Thankfully, the last customer was walking out as she walked in, because this was something nobody needed to see.

"Oh, what a nice surprise! My daughter so rarely comes to visit me," SuAnn said, raising an eyebrow. She walked past Julie and locked the door, before turning off the Open sign.

"Mother, this is not a social call. I have a bone to pick with you. Actually, I have several bones to pick with you. In fact, I have an entire skeleton to pick with you!" Julie had been mad a lot in the last couple of years, but right now she was purely livid.

"What on earth has got you all agitated?" SuAnn stood there, her hair in a perfect bun, her white apron wrapped around her waist.

"You've only been here for a couple of weeks, and you have already wreaked havoc on several people. I don't know how you work so fast."

SuAnn stared at her, like she didn't have a clue what Julie was talking about. "Why don't you sit down and have a piece of poundcake? I think your blood sugar might be low," she said as she walked back behind the counter and started to cut a piece of cake.

"My blood sugar is fine. I don't want any cake!"

"Julie, and don't take offense to this, but do you think you might be going through the change?" Suddenly Julie let out a primal scream.

“Honestly, mother, can you even hear yourself?"

"Good Lord! Don't be screaming like that. I'm new around here, and you're going to ruin my reputation as a business owner. Now, why don't you sit down and tell me what's upsetting you?"

Julie sucked in a long deep breath and blew it out through pursed lips. Janine had taught her that at one point, and supposedly it was a great stress relief. But right now, she felt like an entire bottle of wine was probably the only thing that might alleviate her stress.

"I don't need to sit down. I won't be here long. First of all, it was bad enough when you pressured Colleen to accept a proposal."

SuAnn chuckled. "Young women don't realize that they need to strike while the iron is hot. The young boy asked her to marry him, and he's got a good job."

"Just because he's cute and has a good job doesn't mean my daughter needs to marry him right now. You need to keep your nose out of her business."

"Well, I didn't know it upset Colleen. I'll apologize the next time I see her, although my family doesn't visit me very often," she said, cutting her eyes.

"And then, you go and tell Janine that she should leave town and go chase William. You don't even know William that well. Janine is happy here. She has a successful business, family and friends."

"Honey, we all know that Janine is getting on up in years. She shouldn't have let him leave. There's nothing wrong with moving to Texas and starting a new life."

"You honestly want your daughter to leave when you just got here?"

"Of course not! It would break my heart. But, I want her to be happy. Do you know how many years it's been since I've seen Janine actually happy? And then she finally meets this guy and lets him go!"

"Mom, she's happy. Well, not right now. I mean, right now she's a little sad. But, she had been happy before that."

"Exactly! She was happy because of that William guy. She needed to follow him."

"You're impossible. Forget about Janine for a minute. The worst of your egregious behaviors lately was in the form of you telling Meg to stop going to her group sessions?"

"I didn't exactly say it like that. I told her to stop airing her dirty laundry in public. It's just not classy to tell everybody your problems like that. People are very judgmental, you know."

Julie sucked in another long breath and blew it out, trying to get her heart rate down. "She's struggling with postpartum depression."

"I don't really know what that is. I think I saw a

Dr. Phil episode about that one time. Or maybe it was Oprah many years ago?"

Julie slapped her hands together in front of her mother's face. "Listen to me! My daughter... that's right, she's *my* daughter, not yours... is struggling with depression. You have no idea how bad it's been. Her doctor recommended a treatment plan that included group counseling, and it's helping her. You need to keep your big mouth shut about it, you hear me?"

SuAnn stared at her. She had never heard Julie talk to her quite like that. For a moment, Julie almost felt guilty, but she knew it was warranted and very much needed if her mother was ever going to change her behavior. If somebody didn't knock some sense into her, she was going to ruin everything Julie had built in her new home.

SuAnn's eyes watered a bit, but she quickly used the back of her hand to wipe away the tears before they fell.

"I'm sorry you're so upset at me."

Julie sighed. "Really, Mom? You do understand that's not an actual apology, right?"

"I don't know what you want from me. I'm just trying to help my family. You know, I do have the benefit of many years of living. I'm supposed to be passing along my wisdom."

That made Julie laugh, although her mother didn't seem to mean it as a joke.

"Mom, I know you think you mean well, but the things you say to people are sometimes very hurtful. We all just got used to you being critical over the years, but these are my kids. And that's my sister. And I won't have you saying things that could potentially disrupt their lives."

SuAnn ran her hands down the front of her apron, smoothing it out, and then stood tall. "Well, it sounds like my own family doesn't really want me here in this town."

"Your family wants to have a relationship with you, but not this way. If you can't treat us with more respect and stop interjecting your opinions into our lives, then maybe we won't have a relationship." There, she'd said it. Out loud.

"Well, I'm sorry you feel that way."

Julie rolled her eyes and shook her head before turning for the door. She unlocked it and pulled it open, looking back at her mother who was standing there, staring at her feet.

"We all love you. But, love doesn't mean anything without respect."

With that, she walked out the door and wondered whether her relationship with her mother was over.

CHAPTER 10

As hard as Janine had tried over the years with all of her meditation and yoga and New Age spiritual thinking, she still had a lot of pride. And stubbornness.

As she sat there on the bench overlooking the marsh, she stared down at her phone, her thumb hovering over William's face.

It would be really easy to send a text, ask him how he was doing. He'd been gone for over three weeks now. All she had to do was press the button and act breezy. Act like she didn't really care and was just his friend. Act like she hadn't been consuming massive amounts of ice cream and potato chips every night while lying in a hot bath thinking about him.

The other part of her wanted to call him, hear his voice, try to imagine his warm hand enveloping hers. But, he would be able to hear the emotion in her voice. Would she start crying? Would her voice go up several octaves when he asked her if she missed him and she tried to deny it?

She flipped her phone over in her lap and stared out over the water. As much as she loved the beach, she had grown attached to the marsh also. The tall grass was constantly swaying and moving and bending to the wind. It gave her a sense of peace. She loved when the sun would set, painting purple and orange across the sky, the reflection in the water giving a haunting feeling as day turned to night.

Gone were the fears that a random alligator was going to crawl out of the depths, although she did see the occasional snake. Now, she enjoyed the sounds and smells and sites of the marshland just as much as the ones she loved about the ocean. The whole place was magical to her, unlike anywhere she'd been in the world. It was home.

She felt it so deep in her soul that it was impossible to imagine living anywhere else at this point. And that was why William could never be her boyfriend or husband because he wasn't there. He didn't feel that connection, apparently.

She closed her eyes and took in a long deep breath, slowly blowing it out as she listened to the birds making their last squeaks and squawks of the day. The sound of crickets and frogs and every other living organism that inhabited the marsh helped to ease her mind and calm her soul, but she still felt restless. Sad. There was a sense of longing that she wasn't sure she could assuage.

Just as she was about to stand up and walk into the house to make herself an evening cup of coffee, her phone started to ring. The sound startled her at first as she wasn't used to getting phone calls. She was much more of a text type of person.

When she looked down and saw William's smiling face on her phone, she almost dropped it onto the grass. For what seemed like an eternity, she sat there debating whether to answer it. In the end, she was worried something may have happened, that he needed her in some way.

"Hello?"

There was a long pause on the other end of the line before he spoke. "Janine? It's William."

"I know. I still have you in my phone," she said, laughing softly. It felt good to hear his voice, like a warm blanket wrapping around her.

"I wasn't sure if I should call you or not. I just wanted to hear your voice."

She had one arm around herself as she held the speaker phone up to her mouth. "It's nice to hear your voice too."

"How is everyone?"

"Good. Except my mom is the one who owns that bakery that was opening."

She heard him laugh. "Oh, that doesn't sound good."

"Yeah, it's not good."

"Well, there's always the option to move to Texas," he said. She knew he probably meant that as a joke, but it wasn't funny to her. He wasn't going to be leaving Texas anytime soon, especially if he was still trying to get her to move there.

"So, how's the new job?"

"Good. Our numbers are really looking good, and my boss, Tina, is very nice."

"Tina? I thought you were going to be running things yourself?"

"I'm the manager, but she's one of the vice presidents of the company, so she is going to keep her office in this building and oversee the larger operations."

"That's great," Janine said, getting a sinking

feeling in her stomach. It wasn't that she was jealous. William wasn't her boyfriend anymore, after all. But, even the sound of him speaking some other woman's name made her feel sad.

"I'm glad that you're doing okay, Janine." It felt like he was calling her to try and make himself feel less guilty about leaving.

"Ditto."

She couldn't say anything else, for fear that her voice would break, and she would cry. In that moment, she wished that she could reach right through the phone and pull William back into her world, but that wasn't possible. If he didn't want to be there, she would just have to figure out a way to move on.

"I guess I better go. I'm meeting a couple of work friends to watch the game."

"Oh. I'm glad you're making friends. That's important when you move somewhere new."

"Goodbye, Janine. It was good to talk to you."

"Bye, William," she said, ending the call before dissolving into tears.

DAWSON SAT ON THE DECK, overlooking the ocean as streams of moonlight danced across the waves. It was his favorite place to be at night.

His whole life, he'd been an outdoorsman. Fishing, hunting when he was a kid, riding motorbikes on the trails around the island. Being inside had always been challenging for him, which was one of the reasons why he'd second-guessed his idea of opening The Inn at Seagrove.

But, he was also a people person. He thrived around others even if he did value his alone time. He wanted to get to know people from all over the world, although he wasn't sure how many global travelers would really be coming to his little island.

His favorite nights were when Julie would come over and sit on the deck with him, drinking a glass of wine and talking about their day. But when he had spoken to her earlier, and she had relayed the conversation she had with her mother, he realized she needed a night at home to decompress.

He offered to cook her dinner and bring it to her, but she had declined, opting instead to eat leftover spaghetti and commiserate with her sister for the evening. If there was one thing he had learned about her, it was that sometimes she just needed space and the best thing he could do for her was give it.

So, tonight he would enjoy the deck alone, listening to the waves and preparing for the new guests that would be arriving tomorrow.

So far he'd had a businessman from Atlanta, a young family from South Carolina and of course, his most extended guest, SuAnn. She had definitely challenged him right out of the gate, and he hoped he never had a more difficult guest in the future.

"Oh, sorry. I didn't know you were out here," SuAnn said, as if right on cue.

He turned around and looked at her, trying his best to offer a smile. "No problem. It's a big deck."

She laughed under her breath. "It seems I'm not really wanted around here after all."

Dawson recognized someone who was trying to put a guilt trip on him. He decided not to belabor the point, and instead he used his foot to push out the chair for her. She looked down at it for a moment before finally sitting.

"Hard day?"

"Something like that." He'd never heard her this quiet before. She sounded defeated, tired, a million miles away.

"I'm a good listener," he offered.

She sighed and crossed her legs. "I think my family hates me."

He was surprised to hear her say that because SuAnn didn't exactly appear to be the type of person who had a lot of self realization. "I'm sure that's not true."

She looked over at him, raising an eyebrow. "I don't think you're being honest with me."

Dawson crossed his arms over his chest. "Can I ask you something?"

"Of course."

"Why do you make it so hard for your family to love you?"

"What?"

"It's like you do everything in your power to criticize them, make them feel uncomfortable, make them get mad at you. Why do you do that?"

She looked at him like she had no idea what he was talking about. "I don't do that. I love my family, and I'm just trying to help them. Like I told Julie, I'm a lot older, and I have all of this wisdom to share."

"Come on, SuAnn. You're not trying to share wisdom. You're trying to control everything and everyone."

Her eyes widened, and a look of anger floated across her face for a fleeting moment. "That's a very rude thing to say!"

"Maybe so, but true." Dawson turned his head

and looked back out over the ocean. "You know what I like about the ocean?"

"Do tell," she said, dryly.

"The ocean never changes. You can count on it. The waves come in, the waves go out, the tide comes in, the tide goes out. You can count on it every single day, rain or shine. Not like people. Or at least, not like some people."

"What exactly are you getting at?"

"I'm saying that you're kind of like a rabid porcupine."

"Excuse me?"

"Well, the rabies makes you very unpredictable. Your daughters never know if you're going to bite, and if whatever you're going to say is going to be poisonous to them. And on top of that, you've got those sharp quills. They don't even feel comfortable going in for a hug or a nice girls lunch with you because you might poke them with one of your criticisms."

She laughed to herself. "You definitely should not be a writer. That's just about the silliest thing I've ever heard anyone say."

"Maybe so, but I think it's apt. Your daughters can't be close to you because they don't trust that you're not going to criticize them or hurt their feelings. They keep up their guard. And the problem is, you don't seem to realize this, so you just keep doing it over and over again, pretending like you're trying to help. "

"I am trying to help."

"Well, and pardon me for saying so, but if you continue doing what you're doing, you're going to ruin your relationship with your family. And if that's why you came here, you couldn't be doing more things to screw this up if you tried."

SuAnn said nothing. They sat in silence for a few minutes, both of them just staring at the ocean, probably for different reasons.

"So what should I do?"

"Well, the first thing I think you should do is go sit down there on that sand and think about what I've said. Really think about it. Stop thinking of yourself as the victim. Think about what your words may have done to those people you say you love. And if you feel like you've done something wrong, then apologize. Mean it. And then stop doing it."

She blew out a long breath. "That's a lot easier said than done."

Dawson stood up, realizing he was never going to get any more peace on the deck that night. "Probably so. But if you really want a great relationship with your family, you're going to have to do the work because you've messed it up. No two ways about it."

He turned and started walking toward the house. "Dawson?"

"Yeah?"

She smiled slightly. "Thank you."

He nodded and then turned toward the house, never feeling more shocked in his life that SuAnn had just told him thank you. Miracles still happened, apparently.

DIXIE SAT THERE, her hands on both sides of the coffee mug. It was a crisp, October day, but certainly not cold yet. Still, she loved the feeling of the warmth on her hands as they often got cold from her circulation problems.

"So, are you going to tell us why we are here?" Janine finally asked. She and Julie had been sitting at the table with Dixie for twenty minutes, lots of small talk going back-and-forth about the weather and the upcoming masquerade ball. But it was obvious something was going on with Dixie, and that was why she had invited them to have coffee with her at the bookstore after it closed.

"Can't an old lady have coffee with her friends?" Dixie asked, cocking her head to the side innocently.

"I don't know any old ladies at this table, but I do know someone who is trying to keep something from us," Julie said.

"Is this about our mother? Did she say something to you?" Janine asked, throwing up her hands.

"No. Actually, the most I've seen of your mother is her walking by and occasionally waving in my direction. We try to steer clear of each other," Dixie said, with a laugh.

"Then what's going on?" Julie asked.

"Well, I'm trying to work up my nerve to tell you both this."

"You're worrying me," Janine said, reaching over and putting her hand over Dixie's.

Dixie smiled. "No, there's nothing to be worried about."

"Is it William?" Janine asked, concern on her face.

"No. William is doing fine. This is about me."

"Is it about your Parkinson's?" Julie asked.

Dixie smiled slightly. "Not entirely, but I guess you could say it's related."

"Are we going to keep playing this game of riddles or are you going to tell us?" Janine asked.

Dixie took a deep breath and blew it out. "I'm in love."

Julie and Janine sat there, their eyes wide, before both of them broke out into giggles. "Really?" Julie said. "That's fantastic!"

"Wait a minute. I thought you told us you were out there playing the field, dating every Tom, Dick and Harry out there!"

Dixie laughed. "Well, the only one I'm dating is Harry."

"His name is Harry? What's he like?" Julie asked.

Dixie grinned from ear to ear. "He's wonderful. He's funny, smart and so nice. He kind of reminds me of an older version of Dawson. I met him at Parkinson's rehab, and we just hit it off."

"You're sure it's love?" Janine asked.

"Positive. I've only felt this way one other time in my life. Honestly, I never thought an old bird like me would find love again, but then there it was."

Janine smiled. "Nobody deserves it as much as you do, Dixie."

"Well, thank you, honey," Dixie said, squeezing both of their hands. "But there's more."

"More? Are you getting married?" Julie asked, a hopeful smile on her face.

"Oh, no! I said there would only be one man I would ever marry, and I meant that. But, Harry and I have made a decision."

"What kind of decision?"

"Well, neither one of us is getting any younger, and we both have Parkinson's, so we would like to do some traveling before this silly disease slows us down. Harry owns a really nice motorhome, so we're going to be taking a long road trip after the first of the year."

"Dixie, that sounds so exciting!" Janine said.

"I'm worried about the bookstore. Julie, you can't run it all by yourself."

Julie smiled. "Don't worry. We will work it out in plenty of time."

"I don't know what I would do without you ladies. Having you here has given me so much motivation to live my life. For years, I just existed, thinking there was no second act for me, but then I saw that maybe it was possible. I saw you come here to a totally new town, Julie, and build a life for yourself. And then I saw you build a whole business for yourself, Janine. This world is full of second chances, and I've decided that I deserve one of my own."

Julie and Janine stood up simultaneously, each of them walking to Dixie's side. They leaned in and gave her a big group hug.

"Before you leave town with this guy, you know we need to meet him, right?" Julie asked.

"I wouldn't expect anything less," Dixie said, laughing.

"So, let me get this straight. You're not going to be coming to meetings anymore?" Meg asked. They'd been attending them together for the past week.

Darcy, who was decked out in a pair of ripped blue jeans, high heel boots and a black oversized sweater, leaned against the wall of the bakery.

"Those meetings just weren't for me. I'm so glad they're helping you, though. But, we made a big decision at our house."

"Oh yeah? What kind of decision?"

"Well, my husband is going to become a stay at home dad so that I can go back to work."

"But I thought he came here for a job transfer?"

They moved closer to the counter, where they were planning to order strawberry cupcakes today.

She would give her grandmother one thing, she could bake like a professional.

"He did. But he hates it. So, he's decided to go back to what he loves which is web design. He can work from home doing that, and he's already got a couple of clients ready to sign up. So, now I'm going to be on the hunt for a part-time job. That will get me out of the house and make me feel more human again, I think."

"You don't like staying home with the baby?"

Meg couldn't imagine that. She wanted to be with Vivi all the time, especially now that her hormones were much more balanced.

"It's not that I don't want to be there with Hatcher. I adore him. But, I watched my mother lose her identity when she stayed at home with us. She had hopes and dreams and career aspirations that she just gave up. And then when we all left to go to college and got married, she was left there trying to figure out who she was. It was really hard for her. I don't want that to be me one day."

Meg wondered if she should worry about that, but she had watched her mother do both. Although she had been a stay at home mother, she had built a successful online boutique when the girls got older that she eventually let go when she moved to Seagrove.

"I'm happy for you. And I hope you find the perfect part-time job," Meg said with a smile as they walked up to the counter.

Her grandmother wiped a stray hair off of her forehead, blowing up toward it to get it off of her face. She looked haggard and tired.

"Grandma, are you okay?"

"No. I am most certainly not okay. Trying to run this place by myself is going to put me in an early grave," she said. "Maybe I bit off more than I can chew."

Meg started to worry. Her grandmother never admitted defeat.

"Are you hiring?" Darcy suddenly asked. Meg looked at her, her eyes wide, and shook her head.

"I don't think you want to do that," she whispered.

"Yes, I am hiring, but everybody I've hired so far has left a few days later. Do you know somebody who is responsible and can put up with my apparently difficult personality?" SuAnn asked, cutting her eyes over at Meg.

Darcy laughed. "Listen, if you can put up with my

difficult attitude and personality, I can certainly put up with yours."

SuAnn smiled slightly. "How would you like to start tomorrow?"

CHAPTER 11

"And three dollars is your change," Dixie said, putting the money in the little girl's hand. "Now, you enjoy that book about seashells!" She watched as the little girl made her way onto the sidewalk, her mother waiting there and waving at Dixie through the window.

She turned around to get her purse, ready to finally close down the bookstore for the day so she could go spend some time with Harry. Instead, she heard the door open again. As she turned to tell the person she was closed, she saw SuAnn standing in front of her.

For some reason, she felt like this was going to be a showdown from the old west.

"Hi, Dixie."

"Hello. Congratulations on your successful bakery. I hear the poundcake is very good."

SuAnn smiled. "Mind if I sit down and talk to you for a moment?"

Dixie didn't think she had ever heard her be so polite. Curious, she nodded and walked over to the table to sit down.

"So, what can I help you with?"

SuAnn put her hands on the table, laced together, and stared at them like she was nervous. Dixie was not used to seeing this side of her.

"Well, you seem to have a lot more insight into my daughters than I do. I thought maybe you would give me some... advice?"

"Really? You want advice from me?"

"Look, I know I haven't always been the nicest to you, but I really do respect you. I think you're a strong woman, just like me."

"Well, thank you." Dixie didn't know where this was going.

"It's just that I came here because I love my family, and I wanted to be near them. You know how it is when you're getting older and you don't want to be alone."

"But weren't you married? I mean, you weren't alone."

SuAnn closed her eyes and sighed. "Can you keep a secret?"

"Most of the time."

"My husband left me. I didn't leave him."

"Oh no. I'm sorry to hear that. What happened?"

"Buddy is kind of a boring guy. You know, I had all these dreams for what I would be doing in this phase of my life, and he hardly ever talked. He was nice enough, but he didn't want to travel and do fun things together. I like to salsa dance, and he can't dance at all. I like to watch mystery movies, and he only watches those shoot 'em up westerns. We really didn't have much in common."

"But he left you?"

"Well, probably about a year ago, I was getting stir crazy up there in our cabin. I didn't want to worry the girls, so I turned to online shopping. Before I knew it, I had run all the way through our savings, but he didn't know it. I would have the stuff delivered at our local post office, and I'd unpackage it and bring it home when he was asleep or not paying attention. You know, when he was doing yardwork or something like that."

"Oh wow."

"Before I knew it, he found me out. The bank called him and told him that something must be wrong with our account because massive amounts of money were coming out of it. I had all of this stuff stored in a building on our property that he normally didn't go into. I had to confess what I had done, and he was so angry."

"Do you know how much money you spent?"

"Tens of thousands. We tried to have a big yard sale, but that didn't give us back nearly enough money. And then we started fussing and fighting, and before I knew it, I told him that I didn't think we had anything in common. I offered to go to counseling or something, but he chose to leave."

"And so that's why you came here?"

"Yes. I came here because I missed my family, and I wanted to be somewhere that I was accepted. I wanted to start over because I had seen Julie and Janine do that here, and I was so impressed with them. I thought I could do the same thing, and that they would be proud of me for opening this bakery. But instead, I seem to have made everyone angry."

"You know, I didn't speak to my son William for many years. We had a huge falling out with a lot of misunderstandings, and it stole so many years from our relationship. We're closer now, but not nearly as close as we would've been had all of that not happened. Don't let that happen to you and your daughters. You can't ever get that time back."

"Dawson told me that I'm too critical, and that I need to apologize to my daughters for some of the things that I've said. I never mean any harm. Well, I guess if I'm being honest, some of the things I said to you were meant to be harmful."

Dixie laughed. "Thanks for the honesty."

"And I'm truly sorry. I've just been very jealous about your relationship with Julie, especially. But I can see why she likes you. You could've criticized me right now, but you haven't. I appreciate that."

"SuAnn, your daughters love you. You're their mother, not me. But you have to be honest with them. You need to go tell them the truth. And tell them how proud and inspired you are because of them. I don't think they know that."

"They don't?"

"No. I believe they will forgive you, but you have to be sincere. And you have to stop putting your nose where it doesn't belong. I know it's hard, especially with our adult children, not to give advice. But you can't unless they ask for it."

"I'm starting to see that."

"And trust me, you can have a new beginning. I've fallen in love again, and I'm about to go traveling around the country after the first of the year. If I can do it, you can do it."

"I hope you're right. And I sure hope it's not too late with my daughters."

JULIE SAT at the little desk in her living room, overlooking the marsh out back, and continued writing in her favorite notebook. She was still working on writing her first book, something she only got to mess around with in her free time now. Life seemed so busy these days.

Sometimes, she found herself daydreaming, staring out over the marsh grass, thinking about all of the twists and turns in her life. She liked to weave some of those moments into her book, but she also didn't want it to become an autobiography.

As the days grew shorter, and sunset came more quickly, she appreciated those moments where she got to sit and watch the beauty that God created in the sky above the water. Shades of orange and pink and sometimes purple were painted across the clouds, and it always made her feel so thankful for this life she had built.

Just as she was about to close her notebook and start dinner, she heard someone knock on the front door. She certainly wasn't expecting anyone right now. Janine and Colleen were in their rooms taking naps before dinner. Normally, they had a family dinner on Sunday, but since Dawson was usually busy checking in and checking out guests, they had decided to do it tonight, right in the middle of the week. Dawson wouldn't be over until later, but he was bringing a deep-fried turkey that Lucy had made extra.

"Who in the world could this be?" Julie mumbled to herself as she walked over to the door. When she opened it, she never expected to see Buddy standing there.

"Buddy?"

He took off his beige tweed fedora and put it over his heart. "I'm sorry to bother you, Julie, but can we talk?"

She looked at him, confused. "Of course..." Stepping back, she opened the door and then slowly closed it behind her. He stood there, his hat in his hand, looking at his feet. At first, she had been shocked to even hear his voice because the man rarely spoke. It was low and gravelly, and a little more raspy than she had remembered the few times she'd heard it.

"Are you looking for my mother?"

"No. Not really, anyway. I wanted to talk to you."

"What about?"

"Well, if I know your mother, and I do, I don't believe she's probably told you the truth about what happened."

“She said she left you."

He chuckled and shook his head. "I knew she wouldn't tell you the truth. And I like you girls. I'm worried she might do the same thing to you that she did to me. That's why I drove all the way here to look you in the eye.”

"Buddy, I don't know what you're talking about."

"Now, I don't want to badmouth her, but I have to tell you the truth. Your mother took all of the money out of our savings account and did a bunch of online shopping. We lost everything. Well, all except the house, where I'm still living."

"What? There must be some mistake. My mom has never really even liked shopping."

"Well, she liked it enough to spend all of our savings Nearly thirty thousand dollars.”

Julie grabbed the back of the armchair nearby to keep herself from passing out.

"I'm so sorry. I had no idea."

"I just didn't want her to steal your money. Don't give her access to your bank accounts or anything."

"What is going on here?"

Julie turned to see her mother standing in the doorway, a look of shock mixed with horror on her face.

"I came here to tell your daughters the truth about you!" Buddy said loudly. Julie couldn't believe he was talking this much. She hadn't heard this many words from him the whole time she'd known him.

"You had no right to come here and fill their head full of bad things about their mother!" SuAnn yelled back.

"Okay, everybody calm down. Let's all just take a deep breath," Julie said.

"What's going on out here?" Janine said as she walked out of her room. Colleen walked out of hers right at the same moment.

"Buddy came here to tell us that Mom stole their savings and spent it doing online shopping."

Janine's mouth fell open. "Is that true, Mom?"

SuAnn held up her hands. "First of all, it's not

stealing when half of that money was mine. And second of all, yes. I spent a lot of money because I was so bored and needed some excitement. And it was the wrong thing to do, and I regret it."

"Buddy, I think you should go," Julie said, ushering him to the door. She couldn't believe he had driven all the way from the mountains to tell her this instead of just calling her on the phone.

"I wish you good luck with that woman," he said to Julie before shutting the door.

"Oh, Mom. How could you do this?" Julie said, running her fingers through her hair.

SuAnn walked over to the sofa and sat down, her hands in her lap. "Maybe you'll never understand, but I'd like to explain. Dawson and Dixie have both told me I need to be honest with you girls."

"You talked to Dawson about this? And Dixie?"

"Dawson doesn't know what I did, but I did tell Dixie the whole story."

"But you don't even like Dixie," Janine said.

SuAnn laughed. "We are more alike than you might think. And we're good now."

"I'm just going to give y'all some time alone," Colleen said, walking backwards slowly to her room and shutting the door.

Julie and Janine sat down on the sofa and turned toward their mother.

"The last few years, I have felt like a hollow shell. When I first met Buddy, I fell in love with his kind, timid personality. To be honest, I just wanted somebody to grow old with, and he seemed like a good fit. Not everybody has the strength to put up with me, ya know. He let me just be free. But as we were married longer and longer, I got bored. I wanted to do things, go places, but it was like pulling teeth. And I just saw the time ticking away. I realized we just weren't right for each other."

"So you spent his money?"

"*Our* money. And I did. It was a terrible thing to do, but I didn't do it maliciously. Over the course of a year, I just tried to make myself feel better by buying a bunch of stuff. It became like an addiction."

"Why didn't you tell us?" Julie asked.

"You girls were going through your own trials and tribulations at the time. A mother is supposed to take care of herself and not put that on her kids. But then, I saw something amazing happen."

"What?" Julie asked.

SuAnn reached over and held her daughter's hand. "I saw you bravely leave your life in Atlanta behind and come here to start over. You didn't know anyone, you barely had any money. You were able to create a whole new life."

"Mom, if you were so amazed, then why did you criticize it so much? Why did you try to get me to stay with Michael?"

SuAnn paused for a moment. "I think because I was scared of change. If you changed, then it was forcing me to think about my own life. And then I saw Janine come here and reinvent her life too. The more I saw, the more pressure I felt."

"You could have talked to us. This whole time, we thought you were happy with Buddy. And we thought you were disappointed in us," Janine said. SuAnn reached out another hand to hold Janine's.

"Look, I have a really hard time being vulnerable. I didn't grow up that way. In my house, there wasn't a lot of emotion. It's just how things were back then. Anytime I have seemed critical, please know I haven't meant to be that way."

Julie put her hand on her mother's shoulder. "I know this must have been hard to deal with on your own, and I'm sorry we didn't know you were struggling. You just have to understand that we are all adults, and you don't have any right to be critical or give us your opinion unless we ask for it. We have to set some boundaries if you're going to live here."

"I love you girls, and I'm very proud of you. I know I don't say it very much, but it's true."

"How did you buy the bakery if you spent all your money?"

"I didn't exactly spend all of it. I had a little nest egg that Buddy never knew about, you know, just in case I needed to make a run for it."

Julie and Janine laughed. "Poor Buddy."

"Don't you worry. I've already decided as soon as I start making profit on the bakery, I'm going to send him a little something every month. Pay back the money that was rightfully his. That is, if he doesn't have me thrown in jail."

"I don't think he'll do that," Julie said. Janine cut her eyes at her sister, both of them wondering if he might actually go through with something like that.

“I’m also planning to sign the house over to him. That will more than pay him back for what I did.”

“I’m glad you’re taking responsibility,” Julie said.

"You know, that Dawson fellow is quite a catch, Julie. He really had a nice heart-to-heart talk with me. He's a keeper."

Julie smiled. "You don't have to tell me that. I got very lucky with that one."

Janine looked down at her hands. "I thought I had

gotten lucky. But apparently, he didn't feel the same way."

SuAnn squeezed Janine's hand. "I'm sure he'll come around. He knows what he's missing."

The three women sat there, holding each other's hands and smiling. Julie had never felt so close to her mother, and she prayed that this was a new beginning for all of them.

CHAPTER 12

It had been over a week since Buddy showed up unannounced at Julie's house, and the relationship she had with her mother had only improved. Now, they were having lunch most days of the week, along with Janine and sometimes one or both of the girls. Her bakery was growing more successful by the day, and as holiday tourists started to arrive in town, she was getting busier and busier. Meg was even helping her build a website to sell her poundcake across the country.

The addition of Darcy working there had proven to be a good one. Not only was she a good worker, but she challenged SuAnn at any given opportunity. For some reason, that seemed to have kept her under control.

"What do you think about my make up?" Julie asked as she poked her head into the room. She and Janine were at Dawson's house getting ready for the masquerade ball. It just seemed easier to set up all of the make up and outfits there instead of trying to make their way from Julie's house all dressed up.

"It's beautiful, but half of your face is going to be covered anyway with that mask you bought."

"I know, but I doubt I'll wear that thing all night long. I need to look nice underneath," Julie said, dabbing at her lipstick.

"I don't even know if I want to be here. I'm the only one I know without a date. Even Dixie has a man!"

Julie put her hands on Janine's shoulders from behind, both of them looking in the mirror. "Don't give up on William. He just might surprise you."

Janine turned around and looked at her sister. "No, he won't. I shouldn't have done it, but I went to their company website today and looked up this Tina woman. She looks like a freaking supermodel. There's no way I can compete with someone like that, especially since we're so far apart. Face it, Julie. It's over."

Julie poked out her bottom lip. "I'm sorry, honey. I really thought you guys were going to make it."

Janine sighed. "You and me both."

"Everything okay in here?" Dawson called from outside the door. Julie opened it, and he stepped back several steps, putting his hand over his mouth. "You look amazing!"

"Why, thank you," she said, bowing. She hadn't even put on her dress yet, but the little bit of theater she'd done in high school had given her enough experience creating make up for a masquerade ball.

Dawson was wearing a suit and looked absolutely dashing, of course. "People should be starting to arrive soon. Meg, Christian and the baby are already downstairs. Vivi looks absolutely adorable in her little dress."

"Oh, I have to come down and get some pictures. Let me just get my dress on, and I'll be right there."

Julie shut the door and noticed Janine sitting there, looking down at her phone. "I have got to snap out of this! I can't continue putting my life on hold thinking about him. Tonight has to be a new start for me."

Julie squeezed her shoulders. "I'll support you with whatever you think is best."

"I know you will," Janine said, tilting her head back and looking up at her sister. "You better get your dress on and get down there before the place gets packed with people. Everyone's going to want to squeeze Vivi's little cheeks."

"That's very true," Julie said. She quickly slipped on her dress and shoes, checked her makeup one more time and then left the room.

As Janine stared at herself in the mirror, her makeup almost complete, she made a vow to herself that tonight was the start of something new. She would be open to whatever came her way. Who knew? Maybe there was a new love of her life that would be coming to the masquerade ball.

When Janine finally got downstairs, the place was packed with people. After a difficult time with some glue on eyelashes, she had been delayed in getting to the party. She couldn't believe how many people were there, most of them out on the deck overlooking the ocean. Dawson and his party planner had done a wonderful job of decorating the place. The DJ was playing music, and the table was full of catered food from one of the local restaurants.

"Janine!" Dixie called from across the dance floor.

She was holding hands with an older man, both of them decked out in flashy masquerade ball attire.

"Oh, hey, Dixie."

"I wanted you to meet Harry." Dixie beamed with pride as she watched Harry shake Janine's hand.

"So nice to meet you. I've heard nothing but wonderful things about you."

Harry smiled. "It's great to meet you. Dixie absolutely adores you and your sister."

"Well, I hope you two enjoy this romantic night," Janine said, smiling. She really was happy for Dixie.

As she walked across the floor, she ran into Colleen and Tucker first. They were slow dancing, staring into each others eye's. Janine missed that feeling.

No. No, she was not going there. Tonight was a new night, a new beginning. She was going to be open to whatever the universe had for her.

Then she saw Meg, Christian and the baby sitting on the rock wall near the edge of the deck, watching everyone dance. They were cuddling with Vivi, watching her coo and smile. Janine wanted to see Vivi, but she didn't want to interrupt the precious family moment. Meg was doing so much better than she had been a few weeks ago, and it was heartwarming to watch her become a real mother.

Then she turned to see Dawson and Julie standing at the edge of the dance floor, feeding each other stuffed mushrooms and laughing. Her sister had never been happier than right now, and she was so excited for her. But still, she felt let down. Hollow. Left behind.

How was it that everyone had found love, and she was standing here alone? She thought she had it, and then it slipped right through her fingers.

Just as she was about to go back in the house and go upstairs to hide away from everyone, someone tapped her on the back. It was a man, dressed in a tuxedo, his full mask pulled down over most of his face. He kind of reminded her of the Phantom of the Opera.

"Yes?" She didn't recognize him, so she figured he was going to ask her where the bathroom was or something.

"Sorry if I'm being too forward," he said, his British accent catching her by surprise. "But I was wondering if you might like to dance with me?"

For a moment, she thought about saying no. She wasn't really in the mood, to be honest. She wanted to go raid Dawson's refrigerator and hide upstairs until everyone left.

"Sure. I would be delighted," she heard herself

saying. The man, who was wearing gloves, took her hand and pulled her out to the dance floor.

She slipped her hands around his neck as he slid his arms around her waist, and they begin to sway back-and-forth to the music. Almost immediately, she felt comfortable with him. She couldn't see his face, and she could only smell his cologne, but for some reason she didn't feel at all weird about dancing with a stranger. Maybe she would be good at this whole new beginning thing.

"What's your name?" she asked, rather loudly, over the music.

"Chester."

Chester? What kind of romantic name was Chester? She decided maybe that was a common British name, although she didn't think so. He certainly wouldn’t be the lead in a romance novel with a name like Chester, though.

"I'm Janine. Do you live around here?"

"Actually, no. I just got to town today."

She continued swaying to the music, confused by his answer but enjoying the fact that anyone wanted to dance with her.

Of course, for all she knew, she could be dancing with a serial killer, so she would definitely stay in a public space with him.

In a way, he reminded her of William. They were about the same height, but this guy was quite a bit… chubbier… than her William. As soon as she thought it, she mentally slapped herself. How was she ever going to get over him if she kept comparing every guy to William?

"Can I ask you a question?"

"Of course," she said.

"How is it that a beautiful woman like yourself was out there standing alone on the dance floor?"

She smiled. "I recently went through a break up."

"Somebody broke up with you? He must be an idiot."

She laughed. "Not really. We just wanted different things."

"And what do you want?"

"I want to stay here with my family and friends and build the life of my dreams."

"Seems reasonable. And what did this gentleman want?"

"He wanted… something else. I really don't want to talk about it, especially with a stranger. No offense."

"None taken."

The song changed, but he didn't make any move to break apart. Instead, they continued dancing, both of them being quiet as they just enjoyed the moment. Maybe he would ask her on a date, and maybe she would say yes. She wasn't really sure. Until he took his mask off, she didn't even know who this guy was.

"Can I ask you another question?"

"Sure," she said.

"What if the idiot came back? Would you be with him again?"

She thought for a long moment. "That's kind of personal."

"We're just getting to know each other. I promise I won't tell anyone," he said, chuckling.

She thought for a moment, wanting to choose her words carefully. "I guess that would depend on why he came back. I don't want to be anyone's second choice."

Suddenly, the music stopped and the DJ started speaking.

"Okay, everybody, it's that time of the night where those wearing masks will reveal themselves! On the count of three, take off your mask!"

Janine didn't know if this was a normal part of a masquerade ball since she had never been to one, but she reached up as the DJ counted down and slowly peeled off the mask that was covering the upper half of her face.

But the man she was dancing with just stood there, not moving. It was obvious he hadn't been prepared for that announcement.

"Are you going to remove your mask?" she said to him quietly as everyone stared.

"I didn't plan on it," he said.

"I think everyone is waiting for you," she whispered.

"Let's give him some encouragement! Take off your mask!" The DJ said, clapping as everyone repeated the chant.

Instead of taking off the mask, the man trotted towards the house. Thankfully, the DJ, a questioning look on his face, let it go. He returned to playing the music while everyone got back to dancing.

Janine stood there for a moment, unsure of what to do. Obviously she didn't know this guy, but she felt bad that he ran off.

Against her better judgment, she walked quickly towards the house, looking around outside to see if she could find him. Finally, she realized he had gone into the inn.

She opened the door and walked into the living room to find him standing there, facing the fireplace.

"You know, I've seen Phantom of the Opera. This is feeling a little bit like that."

Still facing the fireplace, he reached up and started to remove the mask from his face. When he turned around, she almost fainted.

"William?"

"Hey, Janine."

She shook her head, her eyebrows furrowed together. "I don't understand. You have a British accent. How are you standing here?"

He smiled. "One of my best friends from high school was British. He taught me well."

“And you’re…”

“Fatter? Yeah, I padded my suit so you wouldn’t know it was me.”

"Why are you here? You're supposed to be in Texas."

“No I'm not. I'm supposed to be here. With you."

She stood there, stunned. "But what about your job?"

“I needed to go and see if I could do it. Turns out, I could. I just didn't want to."

"I don't understand…"

William walked a couple of steps closer. "I love you. I just had to see if I was missing out on something."

"And were you?"

"No. Everything I will ever want or need is standing right here in front of me. It just took me being a giant horses butt to realize it."

"What about Tina?"

He tilted his head. "Tina? She was my boss."

"I saw her picture."

"Yeah. She does look a little bit like a Barbie doll or a high school cheerleader, but she's not my type."

"She's not?"

He walked closer, taking both of her hands. "Nobody compares to you, Janine."

"What about your job? What are you going to do?"

"I resigned. Gave up my apartment. Snuck back into town overnight. My mom doesn't even know I'm here."

Janine smiled. "So you're back? For good?"

"I am. And I'll need your support opening my own company. That is, if you're willing to try this again?"

Janine paused. "I don't know." She turned and sat down on the sofa.

"You don't know?"

"You left, William. I felt like I didn't even matter to you."

He joined her on the sofa, only a few feet between them. "You do matter to me, Janine, or else I wouldn't be here right now. Almost as soon as my feet hit the ground in Texas, I knew I'd made a mistake. Nothing felt right."

"I get that, but the fact that you left in the first place still hurts. Your job mattered more to you than I did. How do I know that won't happen again? What if some other great opportunity comes along? What if you suddenly decide you don't want to live here anymore?"

He took both of her hands. "I was never leaving *you*. I just needed to see if I could do it. I had never been offered such a big opportunity before, and selfishly, I took it. Now I know that my future is sitting right here on the couch with me. Wherever you are is where I'll be. I can build my business right here in Seagrove, and now I know I don't need some boss or company giving me praise. I just need *you*."

A tear rolled down her cheek. "You're sure?"

He smiled. "I've never been so sure of anything in my life."

Janine lunged forward and hugged him tightly. "I missed you so much!"

"I'm never going anywhere again," he said, pressing his lips into her curly hair.

She pulled back and looked at him. “Good, because I’m stealing your luggage.”

VISIT my website and store at store.RachelHannaAuthor.com.